T0095239

The Skylars

BOOK TWO
A New Beginning

D. E. Miller

authorHOUSE®

AuthorHouse™
1663 Liberty Drive
Bloomington, IN 47403
www.authorhouse.com
Phone: 1-800-839-8640

Published by AuthorHouse 1/19/2012

ISBN: 978-1-4685-4087-1 (sc)
ISBN: 978-1-4685-4085-7 (e)

Library of Congress Control Number: 2012900339

CHAPTER ONE

IT WAS A CLEAR BEAUTIFUL morning, with a slight breeze whispering in the trees as Macee sat on the veranda drinking her coffee. She couldn't believe it was August already. It seemed like only a couple of weeks ago she, Tyree and Riley had arrived at their Uncle Alex's ranch. Much has happened since they arrived here. Thank God Uncle Alex was okay and in the good hands of Greg Ort. If it hadn't been for Greg, Uncle Alex wouldn't have made it.

The trial for Rusty Gabe and Ralph Leeman was over and done with, and the jury in Hardin found them guilty and they were hung. Lester Belcher was sentenced to a life sentence along with Brink Waters, and they were transferred to the Wyoming Territorial Prison in Laramie, Wyoming. Jack Belcher was found guilty of fraud, conspiracy to murder and for being a ring leader of murderers, thieves and outlaws. His sentence was carried out and he too was hung by the neck until dead.

Thinking of all that happened brought tears to her eyes as she thought again of her parents. They were so young when they were killed, and Macee still couldn't bring herself to forgive those that took her parents from her.

She heard the bunkhouse door shut and knew she had to help Cookie with breakfast. She so enjoyed her morning solitude and was always sad when she had to get busy. Tyree was the first in the dining room and when Macee came in from

1

the kitchen with platters of food to set on the table, he got up and went to her and gave her a big hug and kiss on the cheek.

"Hey, what is this all about?" Macee asked. "I just wanted to show you some appreciation of all you do around here and that you would be sorely missed if you should ever leave." Tyree stated. "And where do you think I would go, Tyree, and why would you say anything like that anyway?" she asked. "I have seen the way Dave looks at you, and I think he is more serious about you than you think. I don't know what his plans are Macee, but as of now you are only sixteen, and I think you should be aware of his feelings. I don't want to see you hurt, and if he is serious, I think it would be best if you wait to marry until you are at least eighteen."

Tyree finished talking, took his cup of coffee and went outside. Macee stood there just staring after him, not knowing what to say or think. She really respected her older brother's opinions and decisions about ranching, but he made her feel as if she didn't have sense enough to control her feelings or the situation at hand with Dave. She started for the door to tell him about what she thought of all he said, but just then Dave came up on the veranda.

"Morning Tyree, looks like another great day." Dave said. "Sure enough Dave," replied Tyree. "I think we should ask Trey and get his opinion on taking the herd to the fall pasture. We can leave them there until October and then bring them closer to home for the winter. The other hands have been putting up hay, so we can feed them during cold wintry months."

After everyone had eaten, Tyree asked Trey about his opinion on what he had discussed with Dave. "I think you are right, Tyree," said Trey, "I'll get the hands together and we'll do it today." They saddled up and as they were leaving, Tyree told Macee they wouldn't be back until supper time.

Macee and Cookie were busy cleaning up after breakfast when there was a knock on the door. She was surprised at seeing a woman standing there. Macee saw that the woman had rented a buggy from the livery and she was dressed in very fashionable clothes, with a parasol to match. "I am sorry, I forgot my manners," Macee said, "what can I do for you?" "Is this the Skylar ranch?" the woman asked. "Yes, it is," said Macee, "won't you come in and have coffee?"

"Forgive my rudeness, my name is Emma Reed and I am the daughter of Cain and Lois Reed, the couple that Brink Waters had killed for the land. My parents sent me to Philadelphia five years ago to attend "Finishing School for Young Ladies". I didn't want to go, but mother insisted, saying she never got the chance to study about etiquette or how to use it and when. I lived with my aunt there and six months ago she passed away. She was my mother's sister, and the only relative I had left. There was no one on father's side, so I had no place to go. My Aunt left me financially comfortable and going through her estate, I found the deed to the ranch which is now called the BWSlash. I guess my mother sent the deed to my Aunt to keep safe for me, knowing I would eventually come across it. When my folks sent me back East, I was just fourteen. I know where my folks settled but I hadn't been this way before, so I am impressed at what Alex Skylar has built here. I guess what I am trying to say, is that I want to come back and try to make my folks' place a working ranch again."

Macee just sat there, looking at Emma, with her long soft black hair hanging loosely down her back, and her eyes of dark brown that showed her inner feelings when talking about her parents and Aunt. She was a petite woman, with a pert nose that had sprinkling of freckles and a very pretty smile. Macee liked her right off. "I am so sorry about what has happened to your family," Macee told her, "we lost our parents about a year ago. They were murdered also. That's why Tyree, Riley and I came here to be with Uncle Alex, so we have a lot in common."

"Everyone is out right now bringing the herd from the high meadows, and to take them to the fall pasture. Why don't you stay and have supper with us? Also, where are you staying?" "I have rented a room at the boarding house for now," answered Emma. "I would love to stay for supper." "Great," said Macee. "It is nice to have a woman to talk to. Let's go and unhitch the horse and let him drink and we'll put him in the corral and hay him. I'm sure when you get ready to leave, someone will be glad to help you with the horse."

It was six in the evening when the hands got back to the ranch. They were all dusty and tired and very hungry. When they were seated at the table, Macee said, "I had a visitor today and I invited her to stay for supper. She'll be right in, so I want all of you to mind your manners." When Emma entered the dining room, all heads turned to look at her, and they all stood up at once. The empty chair was next to Tyree's, so he pulled the chair out for Emma. As she sat down, Tyree looked at the others and they all had grins on their faces, and this made Tyree blush and feel uncomfortable.

"Emma," Macee said, "the fellow that just helped you is my older brother Tyree. Next to him, my other brother, Riley, then Seth Andrews, Dave Steele, Trey Beal, the foreman, Greg Ort, and finally, Uncle Alex. Guys, this is Emma Reed. Her folks were killed for the place that joins Uncle Alex. Let's eat and we can talk after supper."

Tyree was very attentive to Emma throughout the meal. He noticed how small she was, and was very pretty, and laughed and joked and seemed quite at ease with all of them. After supper, Tyree asked Emma if she would like to have coffee on the veranda with him, since it was a beautiful clear warm night, she gladly accepted.

After they were settled in the swing, Tyree asked, "So why is it you came back, Miss Reed?" "I have been living in

Philadelphia with my Aunt, and she passed away six months ago, and I had no other place to go," Emma said, "I need to find out where I stand, as far as the ranch is concerned. I have a deed to the ranch, but after everything that Brink Waters did, I don't know if I have any legal rights to claim the ranch as my own. I came back here in the hope of settling down, and to make an honest living on the ranch. I know I'll need help, and I wonder if you would be interested in filling the position of manager.

First thing tomorrow I am going to find a lawyer and have him look over the deed I have, and hopefully it will prove I am the rightful owner. Think on what I have asked you Tyree, and we'll discuss it later. Now, I need to be going. I really would appreciate your help in hitching that old bay to the buggy for me." "Sure thing, Miss Reed," said Tyree. "Please, call me Emma as "Miss" sounds so old fashioned," said Emma.

When Tyree brought the buggy around, she noticed he had tied his horse to the buggy. Macee came out to see Emma off, and she said to Tyree, "We'll see you in the morning for breakfast. Good night, Emma, and I hope we will see a lot more of you." " I am sure you will Macee," Emma replied.

On the way back to town, Tyree said "Emma, if you need help, I know Dave would be more than willing to help you legally. He is a lawyer and I know he can find out about the deed. Also, we could go riding tomorrow and look over the place, if you want me to go with you." Emma glanced at Tyree and saw what she liked. He was very handsome, with a dark tan and slightly curly hair and dark brown eyes. He was very muscular and always polite.

"If you want to ride with me tomorrow, I would love to have the company," said Emma, "and also you can help me find the boundaries to my place." "I'll come in and pick you up at around eight, and we have a gentle horse I'll bring for you to ride," stated Tyree. "Sounds great to me, Tyree, and I have guessed you know that I haven't ridden very much, so thanks for the offer of the gentle horse, and I'll be ready at eight." said Emma.

Tyree stopped in front of the boarding house and helped Emma down, told her good night and took the buggy to the livery. Jed Peterson, the stage line proprietor was just coming out of the livery and saw Tyree unhitching the horse.

"Hi," said Jed, "sure is a nice night to be out riding, and with such a beautiful girl." "You are right about that," answered Tyree, "but I guess I haven't seen you around here before." "No, sir, you haven't, and I guess my manners aren't too good. My name is Jed Peterson and I run the stage line here. I have been in Laramie establishing a route from Keeline to Fort Laramie, and on down south to Cheyenne, Wyoming. You must be Tyree Skylar, as I have heard a lot about you, and the description fits." "You are right, and I am glad to meet you. When I'm in town next time, I'll buy you a drink," Tyree said. "I'll look forward to that. Guess I better turn in. Good night," stated Jed.

When Tyree left Keeline and started for home, he was deep in thought about Emma. Why did she come back now, and why did she think the deed wasn't good? All the while she had been away awful happenings went on. Tyree was taken in on her honesty and her beauty, and he hoped that what she wanted now wasn't out of her reach. He couldn't imagine that Brink Waters had legal claim to her property, but only time would tell. He would talk to Dave about looking into the legal affairs for Emma.

The next morning found everyone cheerful and looking at Tyree with questioning looks. "Hey, you guys," exclaimed Tyree, "what is the third degree for?" "I guess what we are silently asking Tyree, is, what time did you get home, and did you and Emma have a good time?" asked Riley.

"Yes we did," Tyree said, "and we talked about riding

today hoping to find the boundaries, and have Dave check the deed to make sure it is legal."

"With pleasure Tyree," replied Dave, "and by the way, I have rented a room at the boarding house to set up my law business. I am going there today to open, and put ads in the Keeline Weekly. My business hours will be eight to five, Monday through Friday. If Miss Reed would like to make an appointment, she can leave word with Agatha Montreal, the proprietor of the Montreal Boarding House. Mrs. Montreal said she would be glad to help me in getting my practice started, and I accepted."

"Sounds great Dave," stated Tyree, "and I'll tell Emma today about your willingness to help her."

Macee sat quietly listening to all that was said. She spoke at last and said, "Tyree, why do you think Emma has come back at this particular time? I feel there is more about her appearance here than what she lets on. Please be careful when you are with her."

"You might have something there, Macee," stated Tyree, "I feel there is more to this also than what Emma is telling us. We should all be careful since we know nothing about Emma or what she is really here for."

When Tyree went to saddle his horse, Sky, Riley and Seth came to the corral. "Tyree," said Riley, "please be careful and watch your back. I have this feeling that Miss Reed has more up her sleeve than she is letting on. I just don't want you to get suckered in by her charms."

"I feel the same way that Riley does," implored Seth, "I have been around a lot of women in my time, and believe me they can really make jack asses out of you, and get by with it! Just make sure she is on the up and up."

Tyree stepped into the saddle and said adios, and with the mare, Lady, on a lead rope, headed for town to pick up Emma. He was thinking of what Riley and Seth were warning him about, but couldn't put Emma in the place of a deceitful person, or out to hurt anyone. He really liked her, and until anything else was proven different, he just knew she was only trying to find out if her property was really hers. He would be wary and watchful of her moves, but knew she was not using him in any way, and he felt he could trust her with his life.

When Tyree reached town, it was only a quarter to eight, so he decided to stop and talk with Sheriff Madison. "Morning Sheriff," Tyree said, "looks like things are pretty quiet around here." "Yep," said Sheriff Madison, "but last night was pretty lively. I had to throw a couple of drunks in jail for disturbing the peace, and I ran two more out of town because they thought they could out shoot and outsmart me. They were so into themselves they didn't even know when I helped them on their horses and led them down the road. I took them about ten miles out and told them to keep going, and that I never wanted to see them in Keeline again. Sure was a long night."

"Did you know either of them?" asked Tyree. "No, I didn't, but one of them looked familiar. I'll try and remember where I have seen him before," answered Sheriff Madison. "What are you in town so early for Tyree?" asked Madison.

"I came to pick up Emma Reed, planning to have breakfast this morning, and if it doesn't get too late, we may ride out to her place later," said Tyree. "Why don't you join us for breakfast, Sheriff?" "Glad to, Tyree. I'll meet you at the Trails End Café in about ten minutes," replied the Sheriff.

Tyree went to Emma's room and knocked on her door. "Just a minute," Emma answered, "if that is you, Tyree, I'll meet you at the Trails End Café." "I'll wait here and escort you, Emma," said Tyree, "and I want you to know that Sheriff Madison is going to join us for breakfast." "Oh," Emma exclaimed, "I guess that will be fine." She opened the door and Tyree saw that she wore a brown split riding skirt with a bolero over a white blouse, with brown gloves, and a brown, wide brimmed hat and riding boots with spurs and carrying a quirt. "I am ready, Tyree, and I think it is going to be a splendid day for an outing," she stated. "Yes, and you look lovely," Tyree said.

As they went past the Mercantile on their way to the Trails End, Tyree noticed a young boy sitting on the edge of the walk. He had never seen this boy before, and as the boy looked up at them, Tyree couldn't help but notice the sadness in the boy's eyes. "Emma, did you notice that boy we just passed, and did you happen to look in his eyes?" asked Tyree.

"Yes, I did," Emma said, "and I have never seen such unhappiness in a young person like that before. I wonder who he is and what he is doing here." "Maybe Sheriff Madison will know. We'll ask him at breakfast," said Tyree.

Sheriff Madison was already seated at a table and having coffee when Tyree and Emma entered the cafe. "Sheriff Madison, I think you remember Emma Reed. I know it has been some years since you have seen her, but if you recollect, she went back East for schooling," said Tyree. "By gosh, you are right Tyree," exclaimed Sheriff Madison, "I was a friend of her folks, and I remember Emma as a young girl. I knew her folks sent her back East to stay with her Aunt while she attended finishing school. Golly, Miss Emma, it is nice to see you again." "I remember you also, sheriff," replied Emma, "and I am so glad you helped in finding who murdered my parents. It seems so unfair that they were killed because they owned the land, but I am glad that justice was served." As they sat and ate, Tyree reflected on the death of his parents. It all seemed so senseless that it had happened.

Hopefully Emma and the Skylar's could now put their tragedies behind them and start a new life.

After they ate and were sitting enjoying their coffee,

the young boy that was sitting on the sidewalk came in. He stood and looked around, and they noticed a disappointment come across his face. "Hello, young man," said Emma, "Are you looking for someone in particular? "Perhaps we can help."

"No," said the young boy, "you can't help. I always come in here at the same time and look, but I know she won't be here." replied the boy. "Why not?" asked Tyree. "Because she doesn't know who I am," the boy said.

"We would like to help you if you will let us," said Emma.

"I can't trust anybody, and I don't think you can help anyway," said the boy.

Emma and Tyree looked at each other, and Tyree then asked the young boy, "Would you like to have breakfast?" "I can't pay," replied the boy. "I will be very glad to buy your breakfast," stated Tyree, "and Emma will be delighted if you would join us."

"In that case, I accept." replied the boy. Emma then asked what his name was. "My name is Jeffrey Richardson, and I am twelve years old." "Where are your parents?" asked Emma, not noticing that Jeffrey winced when she asked him. He just stared at her and didn't answer, but went on eating his breakfast.

When Jeffrey finished his meal, Tyree suggested to Emma that they get started, as it was getting late, and they didn't want to be late for the supper that Macee had planned for them. Tyree looked over at Jeffrey and said, "If you want, you are welcome to come to our place this evening and have supper with us. I'll be glad to come back for you around four. What do you say?"

"Sounds great, if you don't mind," Jeffrey said, "I'll be ready. I have a horse I can ride, so no need for a buggy." "Okay, sounds good." stated Tyree.

Tyree and Emma were both wondering where Jeffrey

came from when they left the café and rode on to Emma's ranch. Tyree decided to talk to Sheriff Madison and see if he might know anything about him. It really bothered Tyree that a boy that young should be by himself.

Around noon, Tyree asked Emma if she would like to have lunch with him at the Rocking S Ranch. "I sure would," Emma said, "even though we had a big breakfast, I feel hungry from all this riding. I wish we could have found one boundary marker, but we will have more days to look." After they had lunch, Tyree rode to Keeline and made sure she was safe in her room.

"I will come and pick you up at four, Emma, if that's all right with you," said Tyree. "I'll be waiting with Jeffrey, and I am looking forward to this evening." said Emma.

When Tyree returned home, he went to his room and drew a bath and was thinking of Jeffrey when Macee called out. "Tyree, are you decent? I need to talk to you." "Just a minute, sis, and I'll open the door. What is so important that you can't wait until I come downstairs?" he asked.

"Hurry and open the door; I need to talk to you before supper," replied Macee. When he opened the door, Macee hurried in and faced Tyree.

"Well, Macee, get it off your chest, what you want to talk about." "Okay, Tyree, but promise you won't interrupt me, for this is the utmost, greatest opportunity I will ever have presented to me," exclaimed Macee. "You see, Tyree, there is a building on main street in town for rent, and I am interested in starting my own business as a dress maker. I know I can make a living at it, and I want to be near Dave. He is starting his practice two doors down from where I want to start my business. I need the first month's rent, and I thought if you would loan me fifteen dollars for that, plus an additional ten dollars for material to get started, I can easily pay you back in three or four months. I already have orders for dresses, and I know I will bring in more clients.

You know I can make men's shirts also, and I can advertise in the Keeline Weekly and people also talk, so I know that people outside Keeline will hear about my shop."

"Are you finished?" asked Tyree, "if you are so bent on doing this, I will gladly give you the money to open your shop. Don't worry about paying me back. I think you have earned every penny you need. Just make Riley and me a shirt every now and then. I want you to know I am proud of you, and I want the best for you, so go and do your thing. I also know that Dave loves you, and like I said before, I think you are too young to marry, but then who am I to say what age has to do with it. I trust your judgment, Macee, so that is all I have to say," commented Tyree.

Macee just looked at her brother and tears formed in her eyes. "Tyree, I just want you to know that I love you, and I will never let you down. Thank you for all you are doing for me. I am not planning on marrying until I am eighteen, and Dave knows that too. I guess I better see to supper, and you need to get going before it gets any later."

As she turned to leave, she looked at Tyree and gave him a hug and a big smile, then said, "You are the best brother a girl could ever ask for," she said, and then left the room softly closing the door.

Tyree picked up his jacket and went to saddle his horse. "Hey Tyree," Riley shouted, "Where are you going?" Tyree explained to Riley about Jeffrey and that he invited Jeffrey and Emma for supper, and was going into town to get them.

When Tyree rode into Keeline, he went to the jail to visit Sheriff Madison. "Hi sheriff," Tyree said, "I need some information if you have time to talk." "Sure Tyree, what can I do for you?" asked Sheriff Madison.

"Remember the boy who joined us for breakfast this morning? He says his name is Jeffrey Richardson, and he seems all alone," Tyree said.

"I can't tell you too much, Tyree. I do know his Grandfather raised him, but he passed on a month ago. His name was Jake Richardson, and he had a small place South of Keeline. He had some money, and I understand he left the boy a little money. I don't know who his parents are, or what is to become of him. Maybe Jed Peterson could tell you a little about him. I doubt if anyone else around here knows anything about him," Sheriff Madison told Tyree.

"Thanks, sheriff, I guess I'll see Jed the next time I'm in town. I don't want to be late for supper and I still have to pick up Jeffrey and Emma. See you around," stated Tyree.

Tyree went to the boarding house where Emma was waiting, and as they were leaving the boarding house, they saw Jeffery was waiting with his horse.

"See you are right on time," Tyree told the boy. "If you don't mind Emma, you can wait here with Jeffrey while I get your horse from the livery." "We'll get along fine, won't we Jeffrey," stated Emma. "Yeah," said Jeffrey. When Tyree returned with Emma's horse and helped her mount, the three rode out of town toward the Rocking S. They didn't know that they were being watched with the most longing and hurtful expression that could ever be seen on anyone's face.

When they arrived at the Rocking S Ranch, Riley came and helped Tyree put the horses up. "How is it going?" Riley asked. "Just fine Riley, what are you trying to say?" asked Tyree. "Oh, I was just wondering about you and Emma, and how serious you are getting about her." stated Riley.

"I am trying to see your point of view Riley, and to keep things cool right now. I am trying to figure out why she really wants to come back, but I will tell you, I am getting pretty serious about her," replied Tyree. "She is really a looker, Tyree, and I hope her intentions are good," Riley said.

When they were all seated at the table, Tyree introduced Jeffery to everyone and, after supper Macee took Jeffrey aside and put food in a sack for him to take back to the boarding house. "Jeffrey, if you need anyone to talk to at any time come to me, I'll ask you no questions, but I am a good listener. Promise me you will?" asked Macee. "I guess I can promise you Macee, and thanks," said Jeffrey.

Tyree rode back to town with Emma and Jeffrey and said goodnight. He then went to the stage line and seeing the light still on, went in. Jed was busy with paper work, and when he looked up and saw Tyree standing there he said, "Wow, am I glad to see you. I can now put my work aside with a legitimate excuse. How about we go to the Broken Bow Saloon and have a drink. I'll buy." said Jed.

"Sounds great to me," replied Tyree. As they were walking to the saloon, Tyree noticed a woman standing in front of the boarding house. She seemed hesitant about going in, and quickly turned and walked on down the street to the Last Trail Café.

Tyree asked Jed about the woman, and if he knew her. "I personally don't know her," replied Jed, "but she came in on the stage today." "Do you know her name, or where she came from?" asked Tyree. "Well, I do know she came from Hardin, Montana, but I don't think that she has lived there. From the conversation I have heard, she was visiting someone there. Her name is Maddie Richardson and she is going to be the new teacher," said Jed. "Her last name is Richardson and so was Jeffrey's Grandfather's last name." "Do you suppose that this could be a coincidence?" asked Tyree.

"I don't know Tyree," replied Jed, "but I do know that Jeffrey checks out the Trails End Café every day, and always comes away disappointed."

When they entered the Broken Bow Saloon, there wasn't much going on. They ordered a bottle of whiskey and two glasses and went to a table and sat down. The bat wings flew open and two hard case looking men came in and sat down at the next table. Tyree and Jed couldn't help but hear what they were saying.

"I say, Andy, we need to locate this broad and see where her folks lived, and if we have to, do away with her also."

"Keep your voice down, Gus, we don't want the whole town knowing why we are here or what we are up to," stated Andy. "Sorry," muttered Gus, "I just want to get this over with."

Tyree and Jed exchanged glances and not saying a word finished their drinks and walked back to the stage line.

"Do you suppose they are talking about Emma?" asked Tyree. "Sounds like it to me," replied Jed, "if I were you Tyree, I would watch that gal pretty close." "Think I'll just do that, Jed. Thanks for the company and advice, and I guess I'll get on home. Night, Jed." "Night Tyree, take care," suggested Jed.

CHAPTER TWO

A S TYREE WAS POURING COFFEE, Seth came into the
kitchen. "Came in late last night Tyree, I am not spying,
but am worried about you and Riley when you come in late. I
promised your Uncle Alex I would look after you two. Greg
and Trey are busy with the cattle and other chores around
here, so I volunteered to keep an eye on you two."

"Do you know anybody named Gus and Andy? Just first
names I heard, but I think they were talking about Emma,"
said Tyree.

"I do recall a Gus from the war, but Andy, I don't know.
What's all this about Tyree?" asked Seth. Tyree explained to
Seth what he and Jed had over- heard at the saloon, and that
they surmised it had something to do with Emma.

"I'll tell you what, Tyree," said Seth, "I know where
some of the old outfit I used to ride with is holed up. I'll go
and see them, and I know they'll tell me if they know this
Gus and Andy."

"Appreciate it Seth, but be careful. These two seem to
be pretty wily, and I think they wouldn't hesitate to shoot
anyone." stated Tyree.

Emma had retired for the evening, and as she turned the
lamp off, she thought she heard someone outside her door.
She took down her 45 colt pistol that was hanging by the
door and made sure it was loaded knowing she would not
hesitate to shoot if need be. She saw the door knob slowly

17

turn and minutes ticked loudly as she sat on the bed with the gun pointed at the door. "I will shoot you where you stand if you try to come in," Emma shouted, "leave now or on the count of three I will shoot through the door." "Don't shoot, we're leaving, be aware of this; we will get you Emma Reed, and no one can save you." She heard footsteps receding and raced to the door, but saw no one going down the stairs. She was frightened and wondered what they meant when they said, "we will get you." She had no idea what this was all about or who was trying to harm her. She had to talk to Tyree, and hopefully he could help her figure out what to do.

Early the next morning, Emma went to the livery and saddled her horse. As she was leaving town, she noticed two men lounging in front of the Mercantile. She hadn't seen them before in town and wondered if they were the two that came to her door last night. When she arrived at the Rocking S Ranch, she noticed all the hands were gone, but Macee came out to greet her.

"Hi Emma, what brings you out so early in the morning? Come on in and have coffee, and if you haven't had breakfast, there's still some left that I can heat up." "I think I'll just have coffee, and Macee, do you know when Tyree will be back?" asked Emma.

"I think maybe at noon," said Macee, "he wants to see Sheriff Madison this afternoon on some legal matters, and to see Dave Steele. You know Dave has his own office in town now, and his business is starting to grow. Emma, do you want to tell me what is happening? You look worried about something," asked Macee.

Emma told Macee about the men who tried to break into her room and the threat on her life. "I don't know who they are, or why they are threatening me, but I am scared, and that is why I need to see Tyree," remarked Emma, "I don't feel safe, and I don't know what to do about it. I thought if Tyree was home, we could go over to my folk's place and look around and maybe find some clues as to why these guys threatened me, and why they want me out of the way."

Macee and Emma were sitting on the veranda when the men arrived home around three. Tyree rode up and spoke to Emma. "Sure is nice to see you here, Emma, you been here long?"

"Yes, since seven thirty, and I need to speak to you Tyree," said Emma. "Come and walk with me while I put my horse up, and you can tell me about what is on your mind," said Tyree. Emma told Tyree what took place at the boarding house and being watched as she rode out of town that morning. "Tyree, I am really scared, and I have no idea what these men want," said Emma.

"I think our best bet is for you to stay with us, Emma," Tyree told her, "I will ask Macee if she would be willing to share her room with you, and this way we can keep an eye on you. I know I will feel better if you were here, and maybe between all of us we can find out what these men want, and who they are. What do you say, Emma, will you stay?" asked Tyree. "Oh, yes, Tyree," Emma replied, "I would be willing to sleep in the barn if we only can find out what this is all about."

After explaining to Macee what their plans were, Tyree and Emma returned to Keeline to pick up Emma's things. Macee was glad to know that Emma was to bunk with her, and went to her room to prepare for Emma's return.

When Emma and Tyree arrived at Emma's room, it was a mess. Someone had broken in and all the drawers were emptied on the floor, the sofa was turned upside down, the mattress was off the bed, all the clothes in the closet were on the floor along with the contents that were in a trunk. Emma stood there with the look of defeat in her eyes. She had never encountered anything like this in her entire life. What did it mean? Who wanted her out of the way and why?

Tyree took her hand and told her it would be all right. "Just gather your clothing and personal things and we'll go back to the Rocking S," said Tyree.

As Tyree and Emma put things in order, Emma couldn't understand why anyone would do this to her. What did she have that was of value? She was suddenly fully aware of her predicament and started trembling. Tyree noticed and came and put his arms around her to comfort her. "Emma," he said, "I will always be here for you, and I promise we will find out who did this." Macee would be more than happy to have Emma move in with them. "Okay, Emma," said Tyree, "if you have everything, let's go home to the Rocking S Ranch."

When Tyree and Emma arrived at the ranch Macee ran out and told Emma how glad she was to have her stay with them. Riley and Seth helped with taking Emma's belongings to Macee's room. "Emma, while you are settling in, I am going to help Cookie with supper. Take your time since we aren't going to eat until six," Macee said, "I'll come and get you when we are ready to eat."

"I can't begin to thank you and your family enough for taking me in," said Emma with tears in her eyes, "you are life savers to me, and I will repay you somehow." "Just stay safe Emma," stated Macee, "I know Tyree cares for you and worries about you, and having you here with us makes it easier for him to be sure you'll be safe."

When supper was almost on the table, Macee went to her room and told Emma that supper was on. She noticed Emma had changed from her riding habit to a beautiful blue dress with a white yoke that was outlined with blue lace. The sleeves were blousy at the shoulder and tight at the wrists with six buttons on the cuffs. She had piled her hair on top of her head in a thick braid and had tied a blue ribbon through the braid. The skirt of the dress was full with a wide ruffle at the bottom. Around the waist was a wide white sash. She had on black and white ankle boots that were fastened with buttons on the sides.

Macee couldn't believe how pretty Emma looked. "Emma," Macee said, "you are beautiful and I know the men are going to be staring at you all through supper." "I only want Tyree to stare at me," answered Emma. When Macee and Emma came down the stairs, all the men just stared and all stood up as Tyree seated Emma.

Riley spoke up and said, "Tyree, if you didn't have your eye on this pretty little filly, I can guarantee you and everyone sitting here, that I would chase her down and make her mine."

Everyone agreed, and Macee suggested they eat while the food was still hot. After supper Tyree asked Emma to sit with him and have coffee on the veranda. "I will after I help Macee and Cookie with cleaning up. I am going to pay you back somehow for my keep around here." "Okay," said Tyree, "I will be out on the veranda." Uncle Alex came and sat by Tyree. "Well son," Uncle Alex said, "we haven't had much time to talk lately. Seems like you really like this Reed girl. Do you have any idea what she is here for?"

"As of now, Uncle Alex, all I know is she is being pursued by two men that I am going to see Sheriff Madison about tomorrow. I have no idea who they are, but I am going into town and ask around. Somebody surely has seen them, and if so, might know who they are. And yes, I am "smitten" about Emma."

After the dining room was cleared and the dishes done, Emma went out on the veranda taking two cups of coffee with her. She gave one to Uncle Alex and sat the other one down on the small end table.

She took Tyree's cup and went back inside to refill it. When she came back out, Uncle Alex said he was going in and read a little before retiring for the night. As he turned to leave he said, "Tyree, I have been thinking about these two men. You know, Emma here may have something of importance, such as a deed they want. The men could also be some of Brink Waters left overs, and they could still be working for him."

"You know, Uncle Alex, you may have something there," exclaimed Tyree, "why else would they be after Emma?" "Something to ponder on, Tyree," said Uncle Alex, "you two have a nice evening, and I'll see you tomorrow, welcome to you Emma, and stay as long as you want. I know Macee is delighted to have you." With a good night having been said, Uncle Alex retired to his room.

"Do you want to go riding again tomorrow, Emma?" asked Tyree, "since we didn't get too far the last couple of days. I still want to find the boundaries to your place, and so far we have no idea where they are located." "Sounds good to me," Emma said, "after I help Macee with the cooking and clean up after breakfast. Since tomorrow is Sunday, why don't we ask Dave and Macee to ride with us? I know Macee needs a break, and it would be fun."

"I will do that," said Tyree, "you know Dave is still living here, so I know he would like to go with us. You ask Macee and we can leave here around nine in the morning." "I guess I will turn in and I will ask Macee about tomorrow before I retire. Goodnight Tyree," said Emma.

Tyree didn't say anything, but took her in his arms and kissed her longingly. When he let her go, her cheeks were flushed, and she looked deep into his dark brown eyes. "I do care for you Tyree, and I want this mess cleaned up. I don't want anybody hurt, so I hope everyone will be careful. Maybe when we get to the ranch house tomorrow, there will be answers there for us. It is going to feel strange going into the house again, but I feel we need to do this."

Tyree said goodnight, and watched Emma as she went in. He felt an overwhelming desire for her, and he knew he was falling hard for her.

The next morning was bright and sunny. It was almost

the end of August, and the days were becoming a little cooler. The girls had put together a lunch, and were dressed in their riding habits.

Tyree and Dave had the horses saddled with a canteen of water on each horse. They knew never to go without water, since they didn't know what the day would bring. Tyree and Emma rode side by side with Dave and Macee bringing up the rear.

The sky was a beautiful blue, with a slight breeze blowing. Some of the aspen trees were changing their fall colors of gold, red and yellow. The girls remarked on the beautiful hill sides, and said they did not want winter to come so soon.

When they arrived at Emma's folks' place, they noticed that the yard was very well kept. When they approached the house, the door opened and a small Mexican man stood in the doorway. "What can I do for you Senores and Senoritas?" he asked.

"Senorita Emma?" cried Manuel, "when did you get back, and why did you not come here right away?" "It is a long story Manuel, and I needed to sort things out. Is Rosa still here?" asked Emma.

"I am sorry to say that Rosa passed away two months ago. Of all that went on here, she just wasted away. I stayed here since I have no other place to go. Besides, someone had to look after your mother's roses as you know how much she loved them, and they have done well," said Manuel.

"I see you have taken very good care of the place, and I want you to know how much I appreciate it, and I know Mother and Father would be very pleased." "I would like you to meet Tyree and Macee Skylar, they are brother and sister, and they have another brother, Riley, who couldn't make it today. This is Dave Steele, and he is starting a law practice here in Keeline. I am staying at the Rocking S for now. I feel I am in danger. There are two men who wish me harm, and I feel safe with the Skylar's." stated Emma.

Manuel gave Emma a startled look and then he said, "There were a couple of men who stopped here the other day and was asking about this place. They wanted to know who owned it, and where they might be. I didn't tell them anything, and I didn't know at the time they asked that you were back."

"I just as soon leave it that way, Manuel. I don't want these men to know where I am staying. If they ask you about the owners, just tell them they are away, and you have no idea when they will return home. If anyone wants to know the name of the owners, they can go to the bank, and Luke Richardson, the banker, knows what to tell them," Emma said.

"I think we will go in now if you don't mind Manuel. I have some papers I need to get, if they are still there." "This is still your home, Senorita Emma, and I am very delighted you are back." said Manuel.

Manuel stepped back and held the door open for them to enter. The first thing that struck Emma, was the rocking chair her mother so loved, and her father's desk and chair. Evidently Brink Waters had good taste when it came to fine furnishings, as they were still in prime condition. Emma started through the house touching familiar items and being home, brought tears to her eyes.

She turned to her companions and said," I am so glad you are here with me. It makes it easier for me to do what I have to do. If you want, come with me up to the attic. I hope what I am looking for is still there."

When they all had climbed the stairs and Emma had opened the door, the smell of a dusty room penetrated their nostrils. Macee started sneezing and Dave offered her his handkerchief.

Emma went to the farthest corner of the room, and taking down several boxes she revealed a trunk. After dusting the top of the trunk, she pulled on the latch, but it was stuck.

Tyree went over and after some struggle, the latch opened. Emma lifted the lid and revealed some old clothes, curtains and throw covers. She started taking articles out of the trunk and stacking them on the floor. When she had everything out of the trunk, she asked Dave and Tyree to turn the trunk over. They gave her funny looks that made Emma and Macee burst into laughter.

Emma went to an old desk and picked up a screwdriver, and then she lifted up the right front leg of the desk and retrieved a key. She asked Tyree to pry up the board on the bottom of the trunk until all the nails came loose. Dave and Tyree lifted the board off, and stood it against the wall. There was a door they opened and this revealed a false bottom in which they found a twenty by thirty inch tin box.

Emma took the key and with shaking hands unlocked the box. They were amazed at what they saw. There were ten leather bags, and in each bag there were one thousand silver Spanish dollars.

"I want to explain to all of you about this. You see, my father was half Mexican and half Spanish. His father was a full blooded Spaniard and these silver Spanish dollars were stolen from him. Grandfather had friends in Spain who found where the bags were hidden, told Grandfather about them, and with my father's help, went to Spain and brought the money back."

"Emma, you will never want for anything with all this money," said Tyree, "I am glad that no one found your secret here. What we should now, is to take this to the bank before it closes, and with all of us riding with you I feel we will be safe enough if anyone is curious as to why we came here." "Okay by me, Tyree," said Emma, "I think your idea is a good one, so why don't we get started and you know what? I think it would be nice to have lunch in town. This will be my treat to all of you for being my new friends, and hopefully in one case, more than a friend and I also want to thank you for helping me out today."

As they were leaving, Emma went over to Manuel and told him she would love to have him stay and keep things as nice as he had. "I will be more than happy, Senorita Emma, to stay and work here. Hope you will be able to return soon." Manuel told her. "I will come back soon Manuel to see you. Dave is looking into legal matters for me, and it might be a while before we get answers." Emma told him. "Via Con Dios" said Manuel. "Via Con Dios to you too, Manuel," replied Tyree.

As they rode toward town, they were all alert and watchful if anyone was following them. They arrived in town with no mishaps and went immediately to the bank. Luke Richardson was busy in the back, and teller Tom Sayer was counting bills behind the counter.

"Can I help you?" asked Tom. "We would like to see Luke Richardson if he isn't too busy," said Emma."

"I'll go see if he can come to the front," said Tom. Luke Richardson went up to Emma and told her how nice it was that she came home.

"Mr. Richardson, I would like you to meet my friends. This is Tyree Skylar and his sister, Macee, and Dave Steele. Dave is opening his law practice, and Macee will be our new dress maker." Emma said.

"Nice to meet all of you, and now, Emma, what can I do for you?" asked Luke. "I would prefer to meet in your private office, Mr. Richardson, if you don't mind." said Emma. "Yes, yes, by all means, come on back to my office," stated Luke. When they were all seated, Emma took the tin box from Tyree and handed it to Luke. When Luke opened the tin box he gasped and then he sat down hard at his desk.

"Do you know what you have here?" he asked Emma, "these bags are worth ten thousand dollars, and I hope nobody else knows about this. I really think you should take this to Laramie, Wyoming to the Wells Fargo safe, since they are really more secure than I am."

"If you don't mind, Luke," said Tyree, "we'll leave the coins here in your safe until we can make plans for the trip."

"It will be all right with me for now, but don't take too long in planning that trip. I will be happy when you take them elsewhere." stated Luke.

"It's about lunchtime, and I'm starved." said Macee. They all headed for the Trails End Café and on the way there they saw two men loitering by the Broken Bow Saloon. Tyree had a feeling that these were the two men who had tried to break into Emma's room and came back later after Emma was out to search her room.

As they were approaching the two men, Tyree said, "Hey you two, what is the big idea of scaring this young lady, and what do you want?"

"We don't know what you're talking about," the smaller of the two men said, "and we don't like what you are implying." The other man was wiry, and gave Tyree an unpleasant smile that suggested it was none of Tyree's business.

"I will warn you right now, that if you so much as look at either of these women, I will personally hunt you down, and you will wish you had never heard of Keeline, Wyoming." stated Tyree. "That goes for me also," Dave said, "if I were you two, I would leave Wyoming altogether, and never would want to come back. You haven't seen Tyree in action." The two men turned and walked into the saloon without commenting to Tyree or Dave about what was said. Tyree took Emma's arm and the four proceeded to the Trails End Café.

CHAPTER THREE

AFTER THEY WERE SEATED, THE waitress came and brought them coffee and water.

"What's the special today?" asked Dave. "We have ham and beans with corn bread, fried chicken with mashed potatoes and gravy, served with vegetables and desert," answered the waitress. The men ordered the ham and beans and the women ordered the chicken special.

While they were waiting for their food, they saw the two men they encountered earlier riding out of town. "Wonder where they're going," Emma said. "I don't think they were scared off," said Tyree, "so we better be aware of our surroundings. I feel we have not heard or seen the last of them."

"I agree with you, Tyree," Dave said, "they were pretty confident that they are tougher than we are, and that makes for a dangerous man, since they feel no fear."

After they had eaten, Macee wanted to show Tyree and Emma where she and Dave were going to start their businesses.

"Being on the main street will be a big plus for both of us." said Macee, "I can't wait to open up and start working, and the best thing about this, is that Dave and I will be only a shouting distance from each other."

"We better start for home," said Tyree, "Cookie will

have supper ready, and you know how upset he gets if anyone is late."

As they were mounting their horses, Macee saw Jeffrey across the street watching them. She rode over to him and said, "Jeffrey, I have here some fried chicken, potato salad, fresh homemade rolls, and a fine cherry pie. I wonder if you would take this to Jed Peterson and Sheriff Madison, and the three of you can share this meal." "Sure thing, Macee, and boy, will it ever taste good. Mr. Peterson and Sheriff Madison will also enjoy it. Thanks a lot!!"

On the way home, Tyree and Emma talked about what they should do with the money. "I think we should take Luke's advice and deposit the money in the Wells Fargo safe in Laramie," said Emma, "with these two men still lurking around, I would feel better if the money was put somewhere else."

"I think I have a plan" said Tyree. "I'll talk to Jed Peterson about what I have in mind in the morning, but right now I need to talk to Seth and Riley as they will have to help us in my plan."

When they arrived at the Rocking S, Riley came out to meet them. "Been busy here," stated Riley, "we found some strays over near Dead Mans End. We had a time of it getting them here as they are really wild. When we had them corralled, we noticed the brands were not the Rocking S or BW Slash, but L C Mill Iron brand."

"That brand was my Father's brand," Emma said, "he had around one hundred head when I left."

"We'll see if there are more out there, and bring them in," Tyree told her, "in the meantime Riley, you, Seth, Dave and I will go to town early in the morning. We have a problem that we need your help on. We'll leave right after breakfast."

"I'll tell Seth since he and I are bedding out with the herd tonight. See you in Keeline in the morning. Where do you want to meet?" asked Riley. "We'll meet you at the stage station and be on the lookout for two strangers. One is tall and wiry, and the other one is short and stocky. They have been bothering Emma, and I think they are after what we are protecting for her. I will explain to you and Seth in the morning about what is going on," said Tyree.

As Tyree and Dave rode to Keeline the next morning, they were discussing what a great responsibility they had taken on. They kept their eyes peeled for the two men that Tyree had told off the day before. No one could foretell what they might do, or how they would do it. Not knowing anything about them, Tyree and Dave were riding on the defensive. When they arrived at the Stage Station, Jed Peterson was having a fresh cup of coffee. Jed handed them each a cup and said, "Tyree, what are you doing here so early? You seem a little skittish."

"I guess all this business with these two men that want to harm Emma has me a little wary. We are asking your help in this matter Jed. When Riley and Seth arrive, I will tell you all about it, and hope we can work out what I have planned," said Tyree.

After Seth and Riley arrived at the Stage Station, Tyree explained to Seth, Riley and Jed what they found at Emma's place, and that they were going to Laramie to deposit the money in the Wells Fargo Safe.

"First of all, I want to know if you are willing to help. This could end up in a fight, and I don't want anyone getting hurt," stated Tyree. "We want to help, Tyree," said Riley, "and you know I have never backed down from a fight; you can count me in."

"Same goes for me," Dave chimed in. "Okay, here is the plan I have in mind, and I hope it works. First, we will purchase four tickets to Fort Laramie from Jed. Macee, Emma, Riley and Seth will be on the stage. Dave and I will leave today. Riley and Seth will be seen boarding the stage along with the girls, but no one will know they are all traveling together. These two men will assume the girls will be traveling unescorted, so they will become more brazen in their pursuit of the girls," said Tyree.

"When you return to the rocking S, Riley, saddle Emma and Macee's horses and bring them back here. Dave and I will wait for you here, since we have a hiding place for them. Circle around the town and come in back of the livery barn. It isn't too easy to see from the street, and when you return to the Rocking S, take the same route. Jed thanks for all your help. It means a lot that you're not charging Seth and Riley the full trip to Fort Laramie. If you ever have a need to call on us for help, or for anything, don't hesitate to do so," Tyree said. "Thanks Tyree, I'll keep that in mind. Just be safe and watch your back," said Jed. "The stage leaves in the morning at ten sharp, so have the girls here at nine thirty and board the stage and stay on the stage until it leaves. We don't want anyone to know it isn't Dave and me so keep a low profile." Tyree stated.

When Riley returned with the girls' horses, Tyree and Dave left Keeline silently. They were leading Riley's, Seth's, Emma's and Macee's horses down the ravine behind the stage station and traveled slowly from Keeline, so they wouldn't raise too much dust. Dave kept looking back to see if they were being followed, but so far there was no sign of anyone coming.

It was getting late when they arrived at Fort Laramie, and the guard on duty called out," Who's there, and if you're friendly, get off your horses and walk up to the gate." Tyree and Dave dismounted and walked to the gate that opened to let them inside. The Corporal on duty came to greet them, and after Tyree told him they were on their way to Laramie, he said there was renegade Indians on the loose, and advised Tyree and Dave to wait a day or two before going on.

"We can't, sir," said Tyree, "we have horses for our

companions who are coming by stage tomorrow, and they will be going on to Laramie where we will all meet. There will be two ladies on that stage, and one in particular is depending on us for her livelihood." "Do you think the stage needs an army escort?" asked Dave. "I think it would be safer to send ten troopers tonight to Keeline to escort the stage tomorrow," the Corporal said. "Thanks, Corporal," stated Tyree.

The girls, Seth and Riley arrived early at the stage station and boarded the stage. Jed opened the stage door and gave two canteens of water to Riley, saying, "I hope all goes well, and that this business with Emma gets cleared up soon. Wish the stage went on to Cheyenne, but I haven't got that far yet. Luck to you all." The driver and shotgun guard boarded and as the driver shouted to the horses they started at a run, with the cavalry forming a procession behind the stage.

Emma and Macee sat across from Riley and Seth, and Macee said, "Riley, how long do you think it will take us to get to Laramie?" "I think at least three days, and since the stage doesn't go from Fort Laramie to Laramie, this is why we will be going by horseback. Tyree will have our horses waiting at Fort Laramie for us, and that is why I asked you girls to wear your riding habits. The two canteens of water that Jed gave us, will be for you girls," said Riley.

"Tyree is being cautious," stated Seth, "and he figured if those two men saw us get on the stage and head for Fort Laramie, we would continue on to Cheyenne, and hopefully they don't know that the stage line doesn't go to Cheyenne. This way it will be faster and hopefully we have fooled those two men by going across country to Laramie."

"Sounds like a good plan to me," Emma announced, "I just want Tyree and Dave safe and to deposit the money without anyone knowing about it." "When we arrive at the Fort Laramie Stage Station, the driver will pull the stage up to the front door as close as he can get. We will sneak into the barn and go on through to the back door. From there we will go down the ravine to a hidden coral where our horses are. Tyree will have your two small bags along with supplies cached with the saddles as we will have a long ride to Laramie," said Seth.

Just before the stage arrived at the Stage Station, Emma and Macee made ready to get off the stage. The Cavalry was ordered to go with the stage back to Keeline, so this left Seth and Riley in charge if any renegade Indians should happen to become an issue.

"Seth," said Macee, "I trust you completely if we are attacked by the Indians. Uncle Alex has told us stories of how well you fought in the Civil War, and of the strategies you set up against the enemy."

"Well, I will do my best to protect you and Emma, and I am hoping that I won't have to," stated Seth, "besides, Riley is a sharp shooter also, and I am glad he is here with us."

"I am too," remarked Emma, "I know Tyree had our safety in mind when he asked Riley for help along with you, Seth." The driver pulled up fast, and the girls along with Riley and Seth got down from the stage quickly.

They ran inside the barn where they couldn't be seen in the dark, and stood there for several minutes until their eyes adjusted to the darkness, and then Riley spoke softly, "take my hand Macee, and Emma take Seth's hand. I see a light and I am going to walk slowly toward it." It seemed as if an eternity past before Riley said, "be very quiet. I have found the door, and when I open it come swiftly and quietly and bend from the waist as to make no target for anyone to see."

When Riley opened the door, he was glad it didn't make any noise. They all ran down the ravine and came to the corral. Riley's black horse along with Macee's paint and Lady were in the corral along with Seth's favorite sorrel.

After the horses were saddled, the girls found their small

bags and tied them on their saddles. They all mounted and headed South West from Fort Laramie to Laramie.

The day proved to be overcast, which was a relief for the travelers. They knew they had a long way to go, and they didn't want to tire their horses. Seth took the lead with the girls in the middle and Riley brought up the rear.

They walked their horses for ten miles, loped for ten miles and toward the end of the day they walked for ten miles. It was dark by the time the weary travelers found a secluded place to camp for the night. When they dismounted, the girls were stiff and sore, but didn't complain. The night was beautiful with a full moon and the stars twinkling in the sky. Riley knew they couldn't have a fire, so they ate jerky and hardtack for their supper. After they ate, the girls took their bedrolls and spread them a little way from the fire, but close to Seth and Riley.

They didn't have to say what they were thinking, for they all had the same thoughts on their mind. They all hoped they lost the two men they left back in Keeline. Seth took the first watch, nine to one and Riley from one to five. At four thirty, Riley woke Macee and Emma, and they had hardtack and jerky for breakfast. They all mounted, with small groans coming from the girls, and started down the trail. When they had ridden for about ten miles, Riley looked back down the trail and saw dust rising.

"Hey Seth," Riley Shouted, "we have company coming."

"Hang on girls," shouted Seth, "we're going to run to that mountain over there. When we get there, get down fast, take your reins and follow me up that game trail you see. Whatever you do, don't let your horse loose."

With a holler they lit out of there, and those horses were ready to run. At the foot of the mountain they all dismounted quickly and in single file they wound their way to the top. At the top, Seth motioned for the girls to go around him and continue on up. He waited for Riley to catch up.

"Riley," Seth said, "you go on with the girls and I'll wait here and see who we have on our tails. I will come as soon as I think it is safe. If you can, find a safe place to hole up for now, and leave a sign for me, such as, take some rocks and make an arrow showing which way you go. I'll destroy them as I come upon them, so no one else will know where we are." "Okay Seth, if you need me, just fire three quick shots in the air, and I'll be here." Riley and the girls started on up to the top, and it was a struggle for them and their horses.

After they made it, Riley turned to the right and walked swiftly. Ahead he saw big boulders, and as he approached them, he noticed a game trail that went between two of the boulders.

He had Macee hold his horse as he investigated the trail. It went for about a quarter of a mile when he came out on a plateau. There was grass and water here, but with boulders all around. It was wide enough for the horses to go between the boulders, so they led them inside where they unsaddled and Riley replaced the reins with halters using the ropes from their saddles.

This made it easier for the horses to eat and drink. Riley was worried about Seth, and told the girls he was going to go back and see if Seth was okay. "You have your rifle, Macee, and Emma has her pistol, so keep them handy, and if you have to, use them. I will be back as soon as I can. Keep watch down the trail, and if we don't make it back before nightfall, take turns watching through the night. When Seth and I start back here, we will be sure to call out to you." "We will be fine Riley, so don't worry about us," Macee replied.

Riley left quickly on foot and vanished around the boulder. Emma and Macee stood and looked at each other and then Emma said, "Riley and Seth will be just fine. Seth is a top notch soldier and Riley is certainly a scrapper. I think we will all be okay."

"I know, Emma," Macee replied, "but I still worry. Let's

chew jerky for something to do." "Sounds like a good idea, Macee, and I'll take first watch." "Okay, Emma, but don't hesitate to call me if you need me, or if you get too sleepy." Macee took both their bedrolls and spread them on the ground, and as soon as she lay down, was asleep.

It had been a long day, and Emma knew she had to keep awake, so she decided to walk on the grass where there was no sound. The plateau was only about five by eight hundred feet, but was grassy and big enough for the four horses. It was a little past ten when Emma heard a stirring outside the boulders. She checked the rifle and cocked it, ready for whatever might be out there. She faintly heard voices and they were coming closer, so she walked softly to the opening and stood to one side.

"I tell you, I saw them coming this way, and there is no way out of here," said a raspy low voice. "Keep your voice down, we don't want anyone to know we're here," the other man said.

"I guess you're right, but we should have nabbed that girl right from the start, and if we had to, beat it out of her where those Spanish coins were hidden." Emma stood very still and she knew the two men could hear her heart beating. What could she do? If daylight came and the two men were still there, they would surely see their tracks and find them. She just hoped their horses wouldn't give them away, and she had just thought of that when she heard a threatening snarl on top of the rocks. "What's that?" one of the men asked.

"Sounds like a big cat, and right on top of us. Let's get the hell out of here!" She heard them scrambling to get to their horses and listened until they had ridden away. She still stood there for a long time and when she moved noticed she was stiff. Not hearing the cat, she surmised it had left. She awakened Macee and told her what happened, and to be alert for the cat.

When morning finally came, Macee looked down the

trail and saw Seth and Riley coming. She went and woke Emma and the girls watched as Riley and Seth approached them. "Riley, I heard those two men talking last night, and they were real close," Emma said, "I recognized the voice of the one who threatened me at the boarding house."

"Let's eat some hardtack and jerky and get saddled up. We have a long way to go. It will be two days before we get to Laramie," said Seth.

After saddling their horses, they rode cautiously from their concealed position and headed on to Laramie. "I think we would be better off if we cut across country," said Riley, "seems to me if we keep trying to follow this game trail, we will end up nowhere." "You go ahead Riley," said Seth, "and I will bring up the rear. We still need to be watchful."

They all knew that this trip was going to be harder than they first imagined, but they also knew that they had to make Laramie by the next day. They were watchful, and hoping not to run into trouble, but not one of them was prepared for what happened next.

They were riding on the rim of a ravine, and the sky was overcast, when all of a sudden, lightning struck the ground not too far from where they sat their horses. The whole sky lit up, and the thunder clapped loudly around them. The horses bolted and the girls couldn't control them. The rain came down in torrents, and the runaway horses ran down the steep path to the bottom of the ravine with the girls hanging on with all their might.

When Seth and Riley finally got control of their horses, they rode to where they saw the girls disappear. They stopped on the edge of the ravine and looked down. There was a full-fledged flood raging down the ravine, and the girls were nowhere in sight.

"Riley, I can't see anyone down there," said Seth, "do you suppose the girls are okay?"

"I don't know, but I think we should ride on the edge of the ravine and keep looking," Riley said.

Riley and Seth rode along the ravine hoping the girls were safe.

When he finally located them, they were on the opposite bank, drenched but seemed to be okay. "Macee," Riley called, "are you two okay?" Macee called back and said she had twisted her ankle when her horse threw her. Emma was okay, just shaken up. "Stay where you are, and Seth and I will find a place to cross and get to you. We need to risk a fire to get you dry, as we don't need you catching cold," shouted Riley. "Okay Riley," Macee answered, "but hurry."

CHAPTER FOUR

AFTER RILEY AND SETH HAD ridden about four miles they found a shallow place to cross. It was around one o'clock and they knew this was going to set them back considerably, but it couldn't be helped.

When they finally got to the girls, Riley saw that Macee had her boot off, and Emma was rubbing Macee's ankle. "How bad is it?" Riley asked. "I think if we wrap it tight and get her boot back on, she will be okay. It will be painful, but I don't know what else to do," said Emma.

"I'll help you wrap her ankle, Emma," Seth said, "and then I'll help Riley find your horses."

Seth noticed a big red bruise on Emma's arm and cheek. "Are you all right?" Seth asked Emma. "I'll be fine," Emma replied, "I saw this log coming but I couldn't dodge it. I feel lucky it didn't do more damage to either of us."

"Macee, I think that this should do the trick, but if the wrap seems too tight let me know," said Seth, "now I guess I better get going and help Riley. Just stay here until we come back with the horses. I don't think it will rain anymore, so hopefully you can get dry."

Emma and Macee huddled around the fire and they slowly felt the warmth penetrate their bodies. They thanked their lucky stars that they were alive. The last thing Emma remembered after the water hit them was Macee grabbing her and dragging her out of the ravine. It was a miracle she had the strength to get up the bank, with her ankle being bad and drenched to the bone. The rain hadn't lasted for only fifteen or twenty minutes, but it came down fast and hard.

"Emma," Macee said, "I feel we have been more than lucky today. I think this is a sign that we are to live our lives to the fullest and don't put off what we want to do or what we want out of life." "I fully agree, Macee," said Emma, "and I have a lot of plans, as I am sure you do also."

They heard horses approaching and saw Seth and Riley coming back with the horses. "The horses are still a little spooky, so I thought we would rest here for about a half hour. We'll rub them down and that will help calm them," said Riley, "and with Seth's help we will put a bite together with coffee."

"Sounds good to us," said Emma and Macee in unison. "How's the ankle, Macee?" asked Seth.

"It is tender, but I think it will be fine if I stay off it. I sure am glad you are fixing a meal, for I am starved." Emma exclaimed.

After they had eaten and cleaned the dishes, put the fire out and helped Macee in the saddle, they went on following the game trail. They knew they couldn't follow it forever, but it was easier riding for Macee, since the path was smooth. Riley knew it would be only a little while until they would stop for the evening, and he wanted to find a place with a stream to fill their canteens and to soak Macee's ankle.

They had ridden for about ten miles when Seth came across an old prospector's cabin. It was close to eight o'clock and they decided to camp for the night.

"I am glad you girls are all right," said Riley, "even though you sprained your ankle Macee, and Emma received bruises. It could have been a lot worse. It will be nice when Jed gets the stage line completed to Cheyenne, then it would be a lot closer to Laramie. I just thought cutting across here would be shorter."

"It is shorter Riley," said Seth, "we just didn't figure on any mishaps along the way."

"We best get some shut eye, and get up early. We might luck out and get to Laramie by tomorrow afternoon." Riley told them.

The nights were becoming cooler. They hadn't seen any signs of followers, so decided to build a fire. Seth took the first watch, with Riley taking the second watch at twelve o'clock. Emma said she would be up at three o'clock as this would give Riley a couple of hours more to sleep.

Emma had the coffee on and ready just as the sun came up. Macee hobbled over to the fire to warm her hands and accepted the cup of steaming coffee with a grateful smile. "How did you sleep, Macee?" Emma asked. "I slept pretty well," replied Macee, "but towards morning my ankle started hurting like all get out. I wish I had my moccasin slippers to wear, but then it wouldn't help my ankle, seeing as I have nothing to wrap it with."

"You are right, Macee," said Riley, "your ankle needs to be in a splint, as the last time I checked the color wasn't good, and I feel you may have fractured the shin bone. Your boot is as good as a splint right now, so I think we won't take it off again until we see a doctor in Laramie." After a light breakfast, they doused the fire, cleaned the dishes and packed everything back on the horses.

After helping Macee on her horse and making her as comfortable as possible they headed out. Riley took the lead and Seth followed quite a distance behind since he was concerned they were still being followed.

Riley glanced at the watch that had his parent's picture in it, and saw it was only six in the morning. He was hopeful they would be in Laramie no later than two p.m. They were to meet Tyree and Dave at the Sleep Easy Hotel and Eatery. Riley decided to take a short break at noon to let Macee have a rest. She was no complainer, but Riley noticed her color was a little more pale than usual.

As Riley was helping Macee dismount, Seth was riding in fast and told them that he spotted two riders coming fast on their trail. Riley looked around for some kind of cover to make a stand. About one hundred feet from where they stopped there was an upheaval of rocks that they could get behind for some protection. Riley picked up Macee and carried her to the rocks, while Seth and Emma led the horses to the shelter.

After Riley made sure the girls would be out of the line of fire, he and Seth took a stand with one on each side behind the pile of rocks.

When the two men came into view, Seth called to Riley softly, "these are the two that have been hunting Emma, and I don't think they want us to make it to Laramie alive." "Seth, you take the tall ugly one and I'll take the short stocky one. If we can, just wing them. I would like to deliver them alive to the sheriff in Laramie," whispered Riley. "You got a deal," Seth said low.

As the two men came nearer to the pile of rocks, they stopped and studied the ground. "Hey Gus, what do you make of these tracks?" asked Andy. "Looks like one of them gals are hurt, and someone carried her to those rocks over there," Gus said.

Riley and Seth silently moved out of the shadow of the rock and Riley spoke quietly. "Drop your guns and put up your hands high. Don't try to be hero's. My partner has his rifle sighted right on the button of your left pocket flap, shorty, and I might accidently shoot your foot, or hand, or knee or ear, since I am becoming very nervous."

Gus and Andy looked at each other and decided a gun fight wouldn't be worth all the pain that might be inflicted upon them. Riley and Seth took the ropes from Gus and Andy's horses and tied their hands behind their back.

"Hey Seth, I am glad that we didn't have to shoot them" exclaimed Riley. "You and me both," sighed Seth, "I never did like to see anyone bleed, especially from my bullet."

Seth helped Macee on her horse, and then helped Riley with the prisoners. After all were mounted, Riley took Gus's reins and Seth took Andy's reins, and they started once again to Laramie.

At three p.m., they arrived at Laramie and were relieved to see the Sleep Easy Hotel and Eatery come into view.

"You girls go on to the hotel and find Dave and Tyree. Get rooms for us, and I'll be back with the doctor," said Riley. Seth took the prisoners to the sheriff's office, while Riley went to find the doctor.

When Macee and Emma stopped in front of the hotel, Dave ran out to greet them. "Wow, it sure is great to see you two," he said, "Macee, are you okay?" "I hurt my ankle, and Riley went to find the doctor, and Seth is at the jail with those two men who wanted to harm Emma," Macee explained. "Let me help you down and into the hotel," Dave told Macee, "and Emma, Tyree is coming now and I know he wants to give you papers for the deposit on your money.

Emma saw Tyree, and ran down the sidewalk right into his arms. He kissed her firmly on the lips, and then noticed the bruise on her cheek. He reached up and gently touched her cheek then bent and kissed the bruise. "I missed you so much Emma," Tyree said, "I never want us to be apart again. Will you marry me?" "Yes Tyree, I will marry you. Let's go tell the others right now!"

Riley had returned with the doctor, who was looking at Macee's ankle. Dave was sitting beside Macee and holding her hand, while Riley was looking at them with a big silly grin on his face. "Everyone is here, so we can tell them now," Tyree said. "Everyone, Emma and I have an announcement to make. We would like to announce our engagement, and will set the wedding date soon." "Oh, Emma, I always wanted a sister, and I am so glad it is going to be you!" declared Macee.

"Well Tyree, you old scoundrel, congrats," said Riley, "I wish you both all the luck in the world." "Goes for me too," Seth told them. "I think we better help Macee to her room.

The doctor ordered her to lie down and elevate her leg," said Dave, "he put a splint on her ankle, but doesn't want her to walk on it. I am going over to the Trader's Mercantile and see if I can purchase a pair of crutches for her."

"Come on over to the jail when you get Macee settled. I want the four of us there when I ask some questions. Since you are a lawyer Dave, I need your expertise on what and how to go about questioning them," said Tyree.

Dave went to the Trader's Mercantile and the proprietor Jake McFeeney came to Dave's aid in helping him to purchase crutches.

Dave looked around the store and was amazed at what Jake had on the shelves. Dave went back to the hotel and went to Macee's room. Macee was lying in bed and had her leg elevated and she told Dave she wasn't in pain, thought he looked too worried and told him he should rest also.

"Macee," Dave said, "I have your crutches here, and if you need any help now, I will be glad to do what I can for you. I am needed at the jail, so if it is all right with you I'll go there now, but I'll be back before long. I will help you use those crutches too. Emma is next door, and I'll ask her to look in on you."

"Thank you, Dave, and I appreciate all you are doing for me," Macee said, "you know you mean the world to me."

"I know Macee," Dave told her, "and I think Emma and Tyree both know how we feel about each other, I am glad they are going to be married." "I am so happy too, Dave," Macee exclaimed, "it will be great to have a sister, and we know, that our time will come. I love you Dave."

"Same here, Macee," Dave said, "I know we will wed in a couple of years, but that will be best as we will have our business established by then. You rest, and I will be back soon."

Dave walked to the sheriff's office and Tyree, Seth and Riley were sitting at a table having coffee. "Sorry it took me so long," Dave said, "I had to make sure that Macee would be taken care of first."

"Sure Dave, we know," replied Riley, "I've seen the way you two look at each other. You can't fool anyone about how you feel for each other!" "Okay, Riley," Tyree retorted, "let's get down to business.

Dave this is Sheriff Les Atkins, and he is as anxious to questions those two men as we are. Sheriff Atkins unlocked the cell doors and handcuffed Andy and Gus and brought them out to sit at the table.

"First of all," said Dave, "we need your full names stated for the record." "We aren't telling you anything," said the tall wiry man, "we know our legal rights, and you all can go to hell!"

"Real friendly aren't you?" said Sheriff Atkins, "I can keep you here for a long time, if that is what you want, or if you cooperate we can make some kind of deal."

"What kind of deal are you talking?" asked the sort stocky man. "Since you haven't done any physical harm to anyone, your sentence will be light. I know you have harassed Emma Reed, broke into her room, and followed her here to Laramie. I don't know why and that is what we want to find out," said Sheriff Atkins.

"Why not make it easy on yourselves and tell us your names for starters." asked Seth. "Okay," said the tall wiry man, "I go by Gus Preen and this is my partner, Andy York. We both served in the Civil War, and we are trying to find honest work," Gus continued.

"So, who do you answer to now, Gus Preen?" asked Tyree. "I don't think that is any of your business," replied

Gus. "I think it best you tell us," Dave said, "if you don't, we can't help you with the charges I am going to present to the judge. You almost caused the lives of two young ladies by pursuing them, and I will personally see you pay for that. You had no right to put them in harm's way."

"We didn't do anything to them girls," said Andy.

"But you did," Dave came back at him, "you chased them for three days, and that is mental harassment, and physical strain to always be alert, not knowing what is going to happen next. The girls almost drowned because they were running from you, so don't sit there and act the innocent parties on this confession. Sheriff Atkins, I think we need to keep them locked up if they won't talk. I think charges of attempted murder and robbery should be added. When is the circuit judge due?" "I am guessing in a week," said Sheriff Atkins, "sometimes he may be a day or so late, but never exceeds three days."

"Tyree, we need to talk," said Dave. "Let's go over to the Red Bull Saloon and have a drink, and discuss what you have on your mind, Dave," said Tyree.

As the four men started across the street, they didn't notice the young woman watching them. She was a pretty woman in her early twenties, with beautiful olive complected flawless skin. She wore a riding habit, and had just arrived in Laramie. As she was tucking her brunette hair back in place, she was aware of the four men walking toward the saloon from the jail.

She walked to the sheriff's office, and upon entering, she saw the sheriff was seated at his desk, reading a newspaper and drinking coffee.

As she was closing the door, Sheriff Atkins looked up and stared. He had never seen such a beauty, and she carried herself with pride and confidence. "What can I do for you, Miss?" asked Sheriff Atkins. "My name is Tam McFadden, and I have just arrived from Hardin, Montana, where I have been visiting my family. I have learned some disturbing news and wish to find someone whom I can count on to escort me to Keeline, Wyoming."

"I think I can help you there, young lady. As of this afternoon, these two gentlemen and two ladies arrived here, and they are from Keeline. I know the girls are now resting at the Rest Easy Hotel and Eatery. One of them hurt their ankle on the way here, so if you want, you can go talk to them," said Sheriff Atkins. "Thank you Sheriff, I'll do just that," Tam said. When she had gone, Sheriff Atkins just sat there, and contemplated on his life. He had never married, and now was too old for someone like Tam McFadden.

When the guys arrived at the Red Bull Saloon, they noticed the bartender was a little nervous. "Hi there," Tyree said, "hope you have cold beers for all of us."

"Sure, I guess so," the bartender said. He set up four glasses filled with beer and told Tyree it would cost him one dollar. Seth and Dave had found a table to sit at, so Riley and Tyree took the glasses over and set them down.

"What's with the bartender?" asked Seth. "Have no idea, and furthermore, why be nervous around us? He doesn't even know who we are" stated Riley. "He could have noticed us taking Gus and Andy to the jail," Dave said, "and, when we get to the bottom of what these two men are up to, we may have answers we don't want to know about."

"What is the plan now, Tyree?" asked Riley. "I think Dave should stay until the circuit judge gets here," said Tyree, "also, I think Macee would be better to stay here for a while to let her ankle heal some more before she tries to ride home. Now I think Emma, Seth and I will head back home tomorrow after I escort Emma to the Wells Fargo Office.

She has to pick up her receipt, plus she will need a key word in order to draw on the money. She will have to provide that herself. I think that Riley should stay also, as Dave may need help on the way home, and to help look after Macee."

"I think you have covered everyone's needs, Tyree," said Seth, "and I am anxious to get back to the Rocking S to see how everyone is doing. I know Alex has top hands, but Trey needs help in keeping them on their toes." "We'll leave tomorrow at around ten thirty," Tyree said. "This will give us time for breakfast and to get our business done. I also want to talk once more to those two guys in jail. They probably won't talk, but I would like to get something out of them."

CHAPTER FIVE

"**WE MIGHT AS WELL GO** back to the Rest Easy Hotel and Eatery and see how the girls are doing," Riley said. They were walking toward the Hotel, when a horse came down the street running like the devil was after him. The rider was just a blur as he went past the four men.

"Wow," stated Riley, "he sure is in a hurry or he lost control of his horse." When the horse came to a skidding halt, the man fell off in a big heap. Tyree ran over to him with the others following.

"He's been shot," Tyree stated, "Seth, go get the doctor."

Tyree and Dave looked at the man lying there, and noticed he was barely breathing. Tyree noticed he was a Vaquero. He had on the big California spurs with the big rowels, the tapaderos on the stirrups and the sombrero that was tied under his chin. He also had on a black fancy leather vest with silver conchos for fasteners. His leather chaps had fringe going down the sides of the legs and his gloves were leather with long cuffs. He wore two- forty five colts tied down. Tyree noticed that the bullet had entered the front of his chest close to his left shoulder. He had lost a lot of blood, and was breathing shallowly.

When the doctor arrived, he asked Seth and Riley to help carry the wounded man to his office. Tyree told Seth and Riley he would care for the man's horse.

When Tyree led the horse into the barn, he unsaddled him and then found a curry comb and brushed him. The horse stood still and seemed to like it, and Tyree realized the man took very good care of this horse. The horse was at least seventeen hands high, glossy black Arabian born, and very proud he was. After he had taken care of the horse, Tyree took the saddle bags and went through them hoping to find out about this man. There was nothing in the saddle bags but a kerchief, ammunition and hard tack.

Tyree left the barn and went to Doctor Justin Park's office. Dave, Riley and Seth were waiting outside, and when Tyree arrived they told him there was no change in the man's condition. The Doctor had removed the bullet successfully, but the man was still unconscious. He had lost a lot of blood and would need a lot of rest.

Dave told them he was going back to the hotel and check on Macee, and since it was close to suppertime, he would get Macee and himself something to eat and they would dine in her room. Seth said he would stay and wait to hear from the doctor. Riley and Tyree decided to go back to the hotel with Dave.

Seth entered the Doctor's office to see how the patient was doing. "How is he doing Doc?" inquired Seth. "He has gained consciousness and seems to be coherent, so I think he will be fine. He still will need a lot of rest, so I would like him to stay here until he is strong enough to ride," said Doctor Parks. "Can I talk to him now, as I need to ask him some questions," said Seth. "Sure, but don't stay too long," answered Doctor Parks.

"Hi there," Seth said to the man lying on the bed, "my name is Seth Andrews from Keeline, Wyoming, and my partners and I carried you here to the Docs office. Glad to see you are feeling better. Can you tell me what happened to you, and where you are headed?"

"My name Senor is Hildago Montoya Rodriques, I am a Vaquero and I have come from Sacramento, California. I was on my way to Keeline, Wyoming to help an old friend out. I had camped about six miles out of Laramie, and when I started to break camp, these two men rode into my camp. I do not know them, or why they shot me, but I remember I shot one of them, but I do not know how bad he is."

"Looks as if someone doesn't want you to arrive in Keeline in one piece," remarked Seth, "I will help you if you want, as I and my other friends will be heading to Keeline soon. Hopefully you will be better and be able to ride when we get ready to leave. I am going to the Rest Easy Hotel and Eatery now to join my friends, and I will ask them about you joining us on the trip home."

"Thank you Senor, and if I can ride with you, I will be grateful," said Hildago. "You just rest and get better so you can make the trip, and I'll be back later. I will be on the lookout for those two men," stated Seth.

Seth caught up with Tyree and Riley and explained to them about Hildago.

When they arrived at the hotel, Tyree noticed a young woman sitting in the lobby, and seemed to be waiting for someone. Riley was the first one to approach her.

"Hi," said Riley, "are you alone, or waiting for someone?" "I guess I have been waiting for you," the young woman replied. Riley couldn't get over how beautiful she was. The long brunette hair glistened in the sun light, and her steel gray eyes sparkled when she talked. She was tall and slender, and very graceful as she rose to face him.

"I asked Sheriff Atkins if he knew of anyone going to Keeline, and he mentioned you," she said. "Okay," said Riley, "we are the Skylar's and we are planning to go home tomorrow. I am Riley, and this is my brother Tyree. The other gents are Dave Steele and Seth Andrews. Macee, our sister, is laid up with a fractured ankle so Dave and she will be staying in Laramie for a while. Tyree and Emma will be going back home to Keeline, but I'll stay and leave with Dave, Macee and Hildago, if he is up for the ride."

"I am hoping to arrive in Keeline before long," said the young woman, "I have business to attend to, and the quicker I get there the better." "Do you mind telling us you name?" asked Tyree. "My name is Tam McFadden."

Tyree asked Tam if she was any relation to Lee and Jacob McFadden in Hardin, Montana. "Yes, they are my half- brothers. My mother married their father after my father died, and then they had me." Tyree and Riley just stood there, not knowing what to say.

Dave came into the room, breaking the silence said, "why don't we go into the dining room and get something to eat? I am going to see how Macee is feeling. I'll take her a menu so she can order her supper." Riley went over to Tam and asked her if he could escort her to the dining room. "I would be honored to be your guest," Tam said.

When they were all seated, Tam said, "I know you plan to return to Keeline tomorrow, and I wonder if you would let me ride with you."

"I guess it will be okay if she rides with us, if that is okay with you Seth?" asked Tyree.

"Sure, Tyree," answered Seth, "I don't see why not."

Emma came down to join them, and Tyree introduced Emma to Tam. "Miss McFadden is going to Keeline with us, Emma. She says she has business there, and it would be safer for her to travel with us." Tyree said. "I am glad we can help you Miss McFadden," said Emma, "I will be pleased to have a woman to talk to." "Thank you, Emma, and please call me Tam."

After supper, Tyree, Riley, Seth, Emma and Tam went to Macee's room. "Macee, this is Tam McFadden, and she is going to Keeline with us tomorrow. You get better so you can come home soon," stated Tyree.

"Nice to meet you Tam," said Macee, "I hope we see a lot of each other when we all get settled."

"Me too," said Tam, "I want to settle down, and hopefully

Keeline will be the place. You have all been very kind to me, and I hope I can repay you someday."

The next morning proved to be bright with sunshine and clear skies when Emma, Tyree, Tam and Seth left Laramie at around ten thirty in the morning. Emma rode beside Tam and noticed a peaceful look on her face.

"You like to ride, don't you Tam?" asked Emma. "Yes, I do love to ride and I have ridden since I was a little girl. My mother and I used to ride every day, and I miss her now. She died two months ago, but I still ride every day and I always think of her and how she enjoyed riding also."

The day went by swiftly, and as they settled that night by the fire, Tyree asked Tam why it was so important for her to get to Keeline. "I can't tell you right now, but I hope I can straighten things out before it all gets out of hand."

"If you need help," Tyree told her, "just let us know." They started early the next morning, and with the good luck they were having, they hoped to arrive in Keeline within the next two days.

Tyree was wondering about Tam McFadden. She didn't want to talk about her troubles, which was her business, so Tyree didn't want to pressure her. He was curious, but he decided when she was ready she would tell them. In the meantime, she was fun to be around, and Emma liked her also.

After Tyree and the others left, Dave went to see Macee and found her sitting in a chair.

"Hey," exclaimed Dave, "you look comfortable. Are you feeling better?"

"You know Dave," Macee said, "I feel just fine. My ankle feels so much better, so how about leaving tomorrow?"

"We have to stay until the Judge gets here," Dave told her, "and I don't know when that will be. I am hoping in the next few days, and when I get the business done, we can leave. I know Riley is anxious to be going also."

"I forgot about those two men in jail," Macee said, "I know you promised Tyree that you would see these two men stand trial. I'll be patient."

"Thanks Macee for understanding," said Dave, "now how about some supper? I'll go down and bring your meal up."

"No, Dave," said Macee, "I want to go to the dining room and eat in style. You can help me with the crutches."

"Sounds great to me Macee, let's go!" Dave said gleefully. Riley joined them, and Riley told Macee he was real glad to see her feeling better.

"I am grateful that all I received was a broken ankle, and that Emma had only a few bruises. It could have been much worse," said Macee. "I know Macee," Riley said, "you two were very lucky." "How about meeting us here for breakfast Riley, around eight?" asked Dave. "Sure thing Dave, see you two then. Rest well, and a goodnight to you," said Riley. The next day proved to be a successful one. After Dave, Macee and Riley had breakfast, the two men went to the Sheriff's office.

"Just received a telegram from the Circuit Judge," Sheriff Atkins told Dave, "he will be here at one this afternoon, and will be anxious to speak with you."

"Sounds good to me," Dave replied, "Macee and I want to get home as soon as possible, and I know Riley is ready to ride. He wants to learn more about Tam McFadden. Riley and I will be back at one sharp."

When Dave reported to Macee about the Judge arriving at one o'clock, she said she would start packing, and if the business with the Judge didn't take all afternoon, she would like to leave early in the evening. At least they could get a little way before it got too dark.

"Dave," said Riley, "I will go and help Hildago get his things together and we'll be waiting here with Macee when you return." Dave agreed, and then he suggested they have lunch.

At one sharp, Dave and Riley went to the jail and the Circuit Judge arrived at around ten minutes after one. After introductions, Dave told Judge Green what happened with Gus and Andy, and that he was pressing charges against them.

"Well Dave," Judge Green said, "I think we have a case, and I will have extradition papers made out to take them to Keeline. Sheriff Atkins will have an escort to take them tomorrow, and I will let you know when the date is set for the trial so you can testify. Emma Reed will definitely be the star witness at this trial. I think it will be at least two months before we can hold the trial, as I am stretched thin trying so many cases."

"We will be around, Judge Green, when you need us. Thank you for all you're doing," Dave commented. Dave and Riley went to the Rest Easy Hotel and Eatery where Macee was trying to be patient waiting for them to let her know when they were to leave.

After being briefed on what took place with Judge Green, Macee suggested they leave immediately. They all agreed and Riley went to saddle their horses. Dave went to Macee's room and brought her bag down along with his gear. When Riley appeared with the horses, Dave told Macee that he would go to the mercantile and purchase supplies.

"I can go," Riley said. "I will do that, Riley, you still have to pack," Dave said, "Macee can sit here and soak up some fresh air." "I won't be long Macee," Riley told her.

"It feels good to be outside after being cooped up for so long," Macee replied, "take your time, I am really enjoying sitting here."

Dave ordered coffee, bacon, flour, beans and a small beef roast, along with jerky.

"Leaving us so soon?" asked Jake Feeney, the proprietor.

"Yes, we need to get back home, because we have been away much too long. We have enjoyed your town, but it is time to get on the trail," said Dave.

"I understand young man," said Jake Feeney, "as I once was in your boots. When you find a good place to settle, a person wants to put roots down. Hope that young lady of yours is getting along okay. She sure is game."

"Yes, she is," replied Dave, "she is pretty special, and spunky. She hasn't complained once, and now she is more than ready to head for home. It is going to take Riley and myself to hold her back and to take it easy so she won't get too tired and be sure her ankle won't start to hurt. She can be a bit stubborn, so Riley stayed to help me. I think I have everything we'll need, so add it up for me."

After paying for the supplies, Jake Feeney told Dave he hoped they had a safe trip home. Thanking him, Dave walked back to the Rest Easy Hotel and Eatery and with Riley's help, packed the supplies on the pack horse. Riley had introduced Hildago to Macee and explained to her that Hildago was going with them to Keeline.

Dave helped Macee on her horse and he, Hildago and Riley mounted and they were all glad to be riding from Laramie and heading for home.

CHAPTER SIX

MADDIE RICHARDSON AWOKE FEELING A chill in the air. She knew that winter was just around the corner, and she knew also that time was running out. The job of teaching school would be a big challenge, but she had a bigger job she had to handle. As she was dressing she glanced out her window.

She was on the second floor of the boarding house, facing the street. She noticed riders coming into town, and recognized Tyree as the person who rode out of town with Jeffrey a couple of weeks ago. She watched and then looked closer at the woman with the brunette hair. She looked familiar, but she knew she had never met her before. She finished dressing and decided to eat at the Trails End Café.

When Maddie entered the café, she saw the riders that rode in earlier sitting at the far end of the room, and Tyree was talking to the group.

She overheard him say that they were stopping first at Emma's place before going on to the Rocking S Ranch. Maddie had heard of the murders of Emma's parents and felt sadness for her.

As she started toward a table near the door, the woman with the beautiful brunette hair looked up at her spoke. "Hello," she said, "would you like to join us? The food always tastes better when you eat with someone."

"I don't want to intrude," said Maddie.

"You aren't intruding," Seth said, "please come and sit with us." Maddie didn't know what to say or do. She decided it would be nice to sit with them and thanked them for inviting her.

"Let me introduce all of us," said Seth, "on your right is Emma Reed, seated next to her is her fiancée, Tyree Skylar, then me, Seth Andrews, and this is Tam McFadden." Maddie just sat and stared at Tam, not knowing what to say, and was afraid to ask her where she was from.

Finally she introduced herself and said, "I am Maddie Richardson, the new school teacher, and I have been here since last week." Tam sat there and pondered what her next question should be. Emma spoke up and said, "Miss Richardson, how many children are you teaching?"

"From last year's roster, there were fifteen, and they range from first through the fifth grades," said Maddie, "and hopefully with new settlers coming, I'll have more."

After breakfast, Tam asked Maddie if she would mind if she walked with her to the school house. Maddie said it would be okay with her, so Tam told Seth she would be at the Rocking S later.

When Maddie and Tam were alone, Tam said "Maddie, I know about Jeffrey, and I want you to know that Jacob is alive." "Oh my God!" gasped Maddie, "I did not know this. I was told he was killed in the war. What do I do now? I know Jeffrey is here and living at my father's place and now my father is dead and he doesn't know me as his mother. Tam, I need your help. I am so afraid I will lose him now that his Grandfather is gone, and his father never knew he existed, since he joined the army before I could tell him I was expecting. Oh, Tam, I have made a mess of my life, but I can't mess up Jeffrey's. I have to sort things out and try to do the best by my son."

"Jacob is in Hardin, Montana now," said Tam, "and I

know he will want to know about Jeffrey, but I won't tell him, I know you should. I don't envy you Maddie, but you know what has to be done."

"Yes Tam, I will tell him, but I don't think he will be happy with the news. He always told me he didn't want to be saddled with any kids and I really think he meant it," said Maddie, "and now I have my father's estate to look into, and that will bring out all the nasty truth about me. I do want you to know I loved your half-brother and we were going to be married, but then he went to war and that was the last I heard from him. I guess now I will telegraph him and tell him about Jeffrey and hope for the best."

"Good luck, Maddie," Tam said, "and I want you to know I am here for you, no matter what happens. I know Jacob is stubborn, but please believe me, I want to be here for you."

"Thank you Tam," said Maddie, "I need a friend right now, and I feel I can count on you."

Maddie slowly walked to the end of the board walk. Her mind was still on what Tam and she talked about, and as she crossed the street, didn't see the horseman coming at a fast gallop. He barely missed her and jumped off his horse and, caught her as she started to fall. "Miss, Miss Richardson?" Seth asked. "Yes," she answered, "oh Seth!" "I am so sorry I didn't see you coming. "Yeah, I noticed," he commented, "you seemed to be a million miles away. Let me walk you to where ever you were going, that is the least I can do after almost running you down," "It wasn't your fault, Seth," Maddie said, "my mind was elsewhere, and if you want, you can walk with me to the school house. I have papers to grade, and it seems easier to do them on a Saturday." Seth was wondering about Tam and Maddie as he saw them together talking very seriously.

"Tam McFadden seems like a nice young lady," commented Seth, "and you seemed to hit it right off." "Yes," said Maddie, "she asked me about my teaching school here and why I came here, of all places. I explained that my father died two weeks ago, and I have his estate to take care of." "If you need any help, just call on me Maddie," Seth told her in earnest. "Thank you Seth," Maddie told him.

After seeing Maddie to the school, Seth walked his horse to the blacksmith's. "Hey John, can you shoe my horse now, or do you want me to come back at a later date?" Seth asked. "I can do him now Seth, if you want to wait, I can loan you a horse if you want to get on home."

"I think I will take the loaner, as I need to get home today. I'll come by tomorrow and get my horse," Seth said, "thank you John."

On the way home, Seth mulled over what he saw happen between Tam and Maddie. It was the first time they had ever met, yet it seemed as if they had been best friends for a long time. Seth decided it would be better for all concerned not to say what he saw and he was sure that either Tam or Maddie would eventually tell him why Tam came to Keeline in the first place. On arriving at the Rocking S, Seth noticed that Tyree and Emma were not home yet, and then Seth remembered they planned to stop at Emma's place first.

Tyree and Emma dismounted in front of her house, and she marveled at how well Manuel had kept the yard, and the fence looked as if it was just painted. "Tyree," she said, "I think we need to sit and talk about our future, and as soon as Dave finds out about the deed, we should discuss what we are going to do with this ranch."

"Emma, I think whatever you want to do with this ranch will be okay with me," said Tyree, "you know what your father and mother planned here, and I think you need to carry out their wishes." "I know Tyree," said Emma, "but plans and wishes get pushed onto the back burner if there are distractions. I really need your input into making this ranch work."

"Besides finding out about the deed," said Tyree, "we still have to find the boundaries and know what the total acreage is, but right now we best be getting back to the Rocking S. Supper will be served at any time."

"Manuel," Emma said, "thank you for staying on, and I want you to know that Tyree and I will be getting married soon."

"That is great news Senorita Emma," Manuel stated, "he is a very fine man and I wish you both much happiness. Does this mean you will come here to live after the wedding?"

"We are going to discuss that, Manuel," Emma told him, "we have a lot of planning to do, but I think it would be great to come here to live."

"Manuel," said Tyree, "if you need supplies make a list and we will be back tomorrow. We need to go to Keeline and check up on things. We'll stop here first thing in the morning. You can hitch up the buggy and bring back the supplies."

"I will be ready, Senor Tyree, and I thank you." Manuel said.

Tyree and Emma left for the Rocking S, and they had to hurry because Cookie would be mad at them if they were late for supper. After they unsaddled and watered their horses, Tyree led them to the corral where he fed them hay. The two then walked hand in hand to the house, and as they were washing up, Uncle Alex came out on the veranda. "Tyree," Uncle Alex said, "we have the branding done, and tomorrow Trey, Greg and Seth along with my help will push the herd to fall pastures. I Sure do miss Macee, Riley and Dave around here, and hope they get home real soon."

"I hope they will be back by the middle of the week. They are bringing a man who calls himself Hildago Montoya Rodriques back here, and he claims he has a friend that needs his help. He hails from Sacramento, California, and is one of those Vaqueros," Tyree said.

"I wonder who his friend could be?" asked Uncle Alex.

"Guess we'll find out when he gets here," Tyree stated.

"I don't know of any Spanish Mexicans living around here, but then he could have friends of any nationality," Uncle Alex commented.

"We better go in for supper before Cookie gets mad at us for being late," Emma told them.

When they were all seated at the table, Tyree said, "Emma and I are going to be married."

"Wow!" said Uncle Alex, "and when does this happy occasion occur?" "We haven't set the date yet," Emma told him, "I still have some unanswered questions about my place, and when Dave gets back, I hope he will have good news."

"By the way, Tyree," Greg spoke up, "when are the others supposed to be back?"

"I think I'll go into town, if Uncle Alex can spare me, and wire Sheriff Atkins on Riley's departure, and also if Riley and Dave met the Judge. I hope the trial won't be too far off, as we need to plan for the wedding, and to get Emma's home ready so we can move in as soon as Dave gives us the go ahead," Tyree said.

"Tyree," Emma said, "if you wouldn't mind I will ride with you. I can purchase the supplies for Manuel while you do your business. I thought maybe we could then ride out to my place and try to find the boundaries."

"Sounds like a good plan Emma," Tyree said. "I guess I can spare you tomorrow Tyree," Uncle Alex told him, "you do what you have to do." "Thanks, Uncle Alex," said Tyree, "I need to help Emma all I can."

CHAPTER SEVEN

DAVE, RILEY, MACEE AND HILDAGO camped that first night about ten miles out of Laramie. It was a beautiful night with a full moon and the stars seemed brighter than usual. It was September third, and so much had happened since Macee's birthday on May 10, 1876. She was remembering the trip from Hardin, Montana to Keeline, Wyoming. It seemed as if they would never get to their Uncle Alex's.

"Riley," Macee said, "what do you think of Tam McFadden?" "Like, what do you think her business is in Keeline, and why the big rush?" "I really don't know Macee," replied Riley, "but I aim to find out" "Thought so," Macee said with a grin, "and I am sure it will take some time also for you to accomplish this task." "Why sis," remarked Riley, "whatever are you talking about? I do declare your mind wanders in strange places."

"Okay you two," Dave intervened, "I know what Macee is talking about, and Riley I know what you have planned, and I would bet you that Tam will figure it out real soon."

"When do you think we will get to Keeline?" Hildago asked Dave. "Hopefully by this Friday," Dave told him, "I also hope that Gus and Andy will be there in jail when we get home."

"Me too," commented Macee, "those two are scary, and the sooner the trial, the better."

"You are so right Macee," Dave said, "I will be very relieved when those two are sentenced and taken away. I know that Tyree and Emma will rest easier also."

"We better get some sleep and start early in the morning. We have a long stretch to go," Riley told them.

The night was still and they felt a slight chill in the air. It wouldn't be long before snow season, and Macee wanted to be home where they would be snug and warm. Riley awoke at five a.m. and lay there reflecting on what Macee said last night about Tam McFadden. He really was interested in her, and wanted to learn more about her. She gave the impression that she was all business, and whatever her mission, she was confident in finishing what she started.

She was beautiful, with her trim figure and auburn hair. He also noticed how her steel gray eyes looked directly into his as she talked, and he knew he was taken in by her, and he knew that he was feeling more than curious about this woman, and he was going to pursue her and hope for the best.

"It's time to get up, and if someone would get me wood, I will start breakfast," shouted Macee.

"Okay by me," Dave said, and with the help of Hildago, they had a fire going in no time, and the smell of coffee was overwhelming in the early morning air.

Macee fried ham and bacon with biscuits, and after they ate, the men went and saddled the horses while Macee cleaned the dishes and broke camp. After saddling up and making sure the fire was out, they mounted and started out at a fast trot.

There was frost on the ground, and the horses were a little on the feisty side, and they really didn't want to be ridden. Macee was having a little trouble as her ankle was still tender, and to put much weight on it made it ache. Dave came to her aide and took her reins and started on down the trail. She was grateful for his actions and told him she appreciated his help.

"Macee, you are welcome," said Dave, "I just want to see you get home in one piece, and I know that Tyree would never let me live it down if anything happened to you."

"I will be all right as soon as my horse decides to settle down," Macee told him.

Riley and Hildago were riding at a pretty good clip, and they noticed that Dave was helping Macee. Riley rode back and Dave told him that everything was okay, and explained about Macee's horse acting up. "We are making pretty good time this morning, so we can make an earlier camp," Riley said, "and you just rest this evening, Macee, we will cook." Hildago had ridden back wondering what was holding them up and heard Riley talking about the cooking. "I can make a mean tortilla with beans and beef, and I would be honored if you would let me cook," Hildago told them.

"You bet we'll let you," Dave chimed in, "I haven't had a decent tortilla in I can't remember when."

"That's settled then," Macee said, "and I will be glad to just sit and watch."

"Dave, you and Macee take your time, and Hildago and I will find a good place to camp and start a fire and have coffee ready for you," said Riley.

Riley and Hildago took off at a lope, and as they rode they both watched for a good campsite. They had ridden about four miles when Hildago called to Riley. "I think I have found a good place, and there is a nice stream here with lots of grass."

Riley rode over to where Hildago was and noticed a cozy grassy knoll and the fast running stream not too far away. He nodded to Hildago and they both dismounted and started unloading the pack horse. Riley went and found wood for the campfire. After getting the fire going, he started making the coffee.

They had just started to get the makings out for the tortillas when they heard horses coming. Thinking that it was Macee and Dave, they didn't look up, and were surprised when the man said, "Looks like you are going to have a pretty good meal this evening." When Riley glanced at the man, he noticed he had a tied down forty five pistol, was riding a big sorrel horse that was lathered, and his companion was just as rough looking as he was.

Riley knew they smelled of trouble, and he glanced at Hildago who also had the same idea of the two men as Riley did. "What brings you two here, and in such a hurry," asked Riley.

"Well, now, I don't think that is any concern of yours," stated the big burly raw boned man who was the first man's partner.

The first man spoke up and said, "Now Bert, be nice to these gentlemen and we might get a bite to eat.

"We didn't invite you to eat with us," Hildago said, "and I am pretty particular with whom I take supper with."

"Well, aren't we uppity, Mex," Clay said sarcastically, "just who do you think you are anyway?"

"I am Hildago Montoya Rodriquez from Sacramento, California and I am a Vaquero, that is who I am, and I can bet you are running from the law, am I right?" asked Hildago. The two men sat their horses not liking what these two men surmised. They were right but now they had to figure out what to do about them. Clay looked at Bert, and they both knew that these two had to be killed.

Riley in the meantime, was hoping that Dave and Macee would be able to see what was happening before they rode into camp. Riley could see the dust from Dave's and Macee's horses, and knew he had to keep these outlaws occupied so they wouldn't notice the approaching horses.

"Do you mind if we eat first, before you decide to shoot us?" Riley spoke loudly, "I sure would hate to go to the hereafter on an empty stomach. Why not get down and join us?"

"Don't mind if I do," replied Bert. Riley looked at

Hildago and with a small nod to Riley, he picked up the coffee pot, poured coffee in two cups, and as he was handing them their cups of coffee, Riley eased his gun from his holster, at the same time Hildago threw the hot coffee in the outlaws faces. When they grabbed their faces, Riley rushed in, took their guns from their holster, and just as this was all happening, Dave and Macee rode into camp.

"What has happened here?" Macee asked.

"These two are on the run, and they thought they were going to have a little supper, and then dispose of Hildago and myself. We sort of outsmarted them, and I was not going to let them bully us," Riley told her.

"Looks like you and Hildago did a good job on these two, but I feel bad for missing out on the fun," Dave said.

"Let's tie them up, and by the time we finish eating, I would think the posse would be here," Riley said. Hildago was making more coffee, while Riley went for more wood.

Dave made Macee comfortable, and the smell of beans and beef was overwhelming. When Hildago had the tortillas ready, he served Macee first, who didn't waste time in eating.

"Oh my gosh, Hildago, this is the best ever!" Macee exclaimed. After supper and the dishes were done, they were sitting beside the fire when they heard horses approaching. Sheriff Atkins came into view, and was pleased when he saw the two outlaws tied up.

"You did just fine," Sheriff Atkins said to Riley. "I'll take it from here."

"What did they do, Sheriff," asked Dave. "They robbed the Laramie First Bank. They are wanted in Cheyenne for assault and battery and disturbing the peace. A reward is being offered, so I will have it sent to you in Keeline Riley," Sheriff Atkins said.

"Thanks Sheriff," Riley said," it will come in handy. I will split it with Hildago, as he helped me in the matter."

"We'll be on our way now," Sheriff Atkins said, "have a good trip home. By the way, your brother Tyree wired me and wanted to know when you left Laramie, and I told him you left the 3rd of Sept., so they will be looking for you before too long."

"Bye, Sheriff," Macee said, "thank you for letting us know about the telegram. We hope to be home soon."

After the Sheriff and posse left with their prisoners, Hildago and Riley looked at each other and started laughing.

"What's so funny?" asked Dave.

"I think I am just now realizing what could have happened," Riley said, "and Hildago here; he sure is some man to ride the river with. He knew exactly what I had in mind, and didn't hesitate to do his part."

Since it was getting late, they bedded down, and soon all were asleep. Early the next morning, Macee had the fire going and coffee on. Dave got up and went for more fire wood, and helped Macee with breakfast.

"You keep helping me in the kitchen Dave," said Macee, "and I definitely will marry you for more than one reason."

When they had eaten and packed up their belongings, Macee asked, "Riley, when do you think we will be home?" "I have it figured in four days, but if we ride longer hours, we should make it in three days. I don't want to tire you out, Macee, so if you get tired or your ankle starts to hurt, just let us know." Riley told her.

"Let's go then. I am anxious to be home," Macee told him. They mounted and started at a good clip, and felt they would make good time this day. They rode until it was almost dark, and Dave found a grove of trees to camp for the night. It was a crisp feeling in the air, and they all knew it could rain if it so pleased. They wished to be home before that happened. Macee could feel her ankle acting up when it was so cold, but she didn't want to say anything about it to anyone. She knew they would coddle her, and she didn't want that. She also wanted to carry her weight around camp.

They had been on the trail three days now, and would be in Keeline tomorrow. What a great feeling that would be to be home. They couldn't wait.

"Hildago," Riley said, "I would be pleased if you would stay at our place until you find your friend, and if you need anything, just let me know."

"Thank you Riley," replied Hildago, "I will take you up on that invitation."

After a quick supper, they retired early, as they would be getting up early, for they wanted to be home before lunch time. While they prepared to leave their camp, Macee reflected on how lucky they had been, and how nice to see everyone in a little while.

They finally arrived at the Rocking S where Uncle Alex came running to greet them. "Welcome home," Uncle Alex said, "I have really missed you."

Tyree and Emma along with the rest of the gang came to greet them. "Sure is nice to have all of you home," Emma commented, "and to see you getting along okay, Macee, I am so glad."

"I am doing just great, Emma," said Macee, "and I can't wait to get cleaned up, and sleep in my bed."

"I'll come with you Macee and draw your bath," Emma said. As the girls went to the house, Tyree filled Dave and Riley on what was happening with Gabe and Andy.

"Sounds great to me," Riley said, "also, Hildago is going to stay here until he can find his friend."

"Welcome, Hildago," Uncle Alex said, "stay as long as you want." "Thank you Senor Alex," Hildago said, "I appreciate the offer."

After the travelers were settled it was time for lunch, and while they were enjoying Cookie's meal, Uncle Alex told them of the branding and that the herd was in the fall pastures. They still had to check on the herd from time to time, but just to make sure that when calving time came, they would move the herd closer to home.

Early the next morning, after breakfast, Tyree and Emma headed for Emma's place. She wanted to start calling her home the LC Mill Iron, and she hoped she had the legal right to do so. Manuel met them at the gate and said, "I have coffee on plus I made some doughnuts."

"We just ate Manuel," Tyree said, "but I will never pass up doughnuts!" "Me either," exclaimed Emma. They tied their horses to the hitching rail and went inside where the smell of fresh brewed coffee and freshly made doughnuts permeated the air.

Emma went to her mother's rocking chair and sat down. She closed her eyes and imagined the peaceful look on her mother's face as she rocked. Oh how she missed her parents! It all was so unfair, and it didn't matter that the murderers were convicted; it would not bring her parents back.

Manuel called from the kitchen to come and sit down, and when she entered she noticed he had set the table with her mother's lace table cloth with matching napkins and her mother's china cups and saucers and pie plates. Emma was impressed at how Manuel had displayed the setting. He had pansies and mums for the center piece in the vase that her Father had given her mother for their fifth Wedding Anniversary. It was very beautiful. As she looked around at the familiar surroundings, she knew this was where she wanted to live with Tyree and to raise her children, hoping Tyree would come to love it here as much as she.

"Manuel," Emma remarked, "you have outdone yourself. These are the tastiest doughnuts I have ever eaten, and the coffee is delicious."

"I agree with Emma," Tyree told him, "you can cook for me anytime."

"I see you have the buckboard ready Manuel," said Tyree, "so Emma will meet you at the mercantile and get the things you need. I have other business to attend to. Remember, if you need anything, let me know." "Thank you Senor Tyree," Manuel said, "you are very kind."

When Tyree and Emma were riding down the lane to the main road Tyree told Emma he was going to stop and see Sheriff Madison first, as he needed to discuss the arrival of Gus Preen and Andy York, and maybe Madison had some idea as to when the trial would take place. He then would go to the telegraph office and wire Sheriff Atkins in Laramie, wanting to know when Riley and the others left Laramie.

"You have a lot to do Tyree," Emma said, "so I'll meet Manuel at the Mercantile, and then I will head back to my place."

"No Emma," Tyree said, "I don't want you going anywhere by yourself. I still don't feel it is all that safe for you, so just go to the Trails End Café and wait there for me."

"Okay," Emma agreed, "but don't be too long. I have a lot of things to talk over with you." Tyree took her in his arms and kissed her soundly on her lips before he let her go.

"I will be there before you know it," Tyree told her, "and I love you, Emma Reed." Emma blushed and it pleased her that he didn't mind showing his affections for her in public. "I love you too," Emma replied with a grin on her face, "I'll see you soon,"

When Emma had purchased the supplies for Manuel, and watched as he rode out of town, she went on to the Trails End Café. The first person she saw as she entered the Café was Maddie Richardson. "Hi Maddie, it is so nice to see you again," Emma told her.

"You too, Emma," replied Maddie, "it was nice having lunch with all of you the other day. It feels good to talk to adults once in a while, instead of talking to children all the time."

"I am sure the children appreciate you Maddie, and I can only wonder how hard your job can be," stated Emma, "I don't think I would have the patience."

"Sometimes it is a real challenge, but the reward in the end is all worth it," Maddie said seriously, "to see them graduate and make it on their own is such a great feeling of accomplishment on my part."

"I can see what you mean Maddie," Emma told her. While they sat there chatting about the weather, guessing when Macee and the others was due to arrive, Jeffrey Richardson came in and sat down. He looked all around and finally saw Emma and Maddie sitting there. Emma noticed a sadness that came to Maddie's eyes and then she looked at Jeffrey and also thought of how sad he always seemed.

"Maddie," Emma approached her, "I can't help but wonder at your last name and Jeffrey's being the same."

"Oh, yes Emma," Maddie exclaimed, "you see, my father took in Jeffrey gave him his last name, and asked Jeffrey to call him Grandpa. It has been hard on Jeffrey since my father passed away, and I have been trying to help Jeffrey, but he doesn't want anything to do with me. He does come to school, but as far as really sitting down and talking with me, he just clams up and he usually walks away."

"I am so sorry Maddie," Emma told her, "but you know, Macee and Jeffrey seem too get along great, and when she arrives home I'll talk to her about Jeffrey and see what she can do to help." "You would do that?" exclaimed Maddie, "I don't know what to say, but thank you so much." Tyree came in and stopped to say hello to Jeffrey. Jeffrey asked Tyree how the trip was, and after they talked for a while, Jeffrey left. Tyree walked over to the table where the two women sat and said hello to Maddie. "I think I had better go now," Maddie said, "you two have a great afternoon." "You also Maddie," Emma said, "and I hope to see you soon."

Tyree and Emma rode from Keeline at around one p.m.

They decided to ride north from Emma's ranch house and start looking for the boundaries. When they arrived Manuel came out, and Tyree told him that he and Emma were going to ride north to try to locate the boundaries of the ranch.

"I don't know how long we'll be, Manuel," Tyree said, "but we won't come back this way, I want to ride east also. I want to thank you again for all you have done around here, and I know Emma really wants you to stay."

"I have no other place to go Senor Tyree, and I will stay as long as Senorita Emma needs me," Manuel told Tyree.

When Tyree and Emma started up a dim trail, Emma asked Tyree what he thought about calling the ranch the LC Mill Iron, and not only run cattle on the range, but have horses also.

"If that is what you want Emma," Tyree said, "then I will help you get started. You have the cows to start building a bigger herd, and I think I know where you can buy horses."

"But Tyree, I want this to be "our" ranch. When we marry you know we'll share everything, and that means profits and losses!" stated Emma.

"I know what you're saying Emma," Tyree said, "but I don't want anyone to say I'm marrying you for your money or your ranch." "Anyone who knows you Tyree knows you are not that kind of person and I really don't care what people think. Besides, it is nobody's business but ours," retorted Emma.

As they came to the top of the hill, they both were amazed at the beauty of the valley below. The fall colors shining in red, gold, brown and silver. They sat there a long while just taking in the beautiful scenery.

When they mounted and started down the East side of the hill, Emma told Tyree what Maddie and she talked about while waiting for him. "Tyree, I don't think Maddie was telling me the truth about Jeffrey, but then that is her business. I did tell her that I would talk to Macee when Macee arrives home and hopefully she can help Jeffrey in some way to come to terms about what is bothering him."

"I think you have a good idea there, Emma. Macee always liked kids, and if anyone can get through to Jeffrey, I know it will be Macee," Tyree said.

They had ridden about five miles when Tyree spotted the boundary marker. Tyree dismounted and brushed the dirt from around the marker, and he found a thick strong stem from the underbrush, and removed his bandana and tied it on the stem. He and Emma gathered up rocks and piled them around the marker. He then stuck the stem deep in the middle of the rocks they had piled around the marker, and made sure it was secure. He told Emma this would make it easier next time they came to find it.

"I think we should plant a tree beside each boundary, and then as we have children, we can name the tree for them," he told Emma.

"I think that is a wonderful idea Tyree, and if we have more than four children, we can plant more trees," Emma exclaimed. Tyree just looked at her and smiled knowing they both would welcome a large family.

When Emma and Tyree arrived at the Rocking S, they heard music and singing. Tyree asked Riley, "What's the occasion?"

"It so happens that today is Uncle Alex's birthday, so Seth, Greg and myself decided to put on a little "Fandango" for him. He is celebrating his Forty Fifth Birthday today, which is Sept.15th. We hired a fiddler and a drummer and guitar player, and Cookie, with the help of Agatha Montreal, has put together the biggest feast you have ever set your eyes on," Riley said.

"Let's join the fun Tyree," Emma said excitedly.

"I'll help you unsaddle Tyree," Riley said, "while Emma goes and gets prettied up."

"Thanks Riley," Emma told him, "I really appreciate that." She hurried into the house and ran upstairs to bathe and dress. She noticed that Macee had bathed and dressed, and that she was probably downstairs enjoying the party.

As Emma was getting ready, she listened to the music and smiled to herself. She vowed to herself that when she and Tyree were married they would entertain at least once a month. It would be nice to have people round and catch up on the latest news. She went to the closet and looking at her wardrobe, she picked out the green velvet dress. It was one of her favorites. The skirt was tiered with black lace between the tiers. The bodice was form fitting with the neckline shaped in a vee, and black lace at the neckline. The sleeves were made of the black lace with green velvet piping sewn down the outside stopping just above the cuff, which was made of green velvet also. Around her waist she tied a black lace sash, and she tied a black ribbon in the braid that hung down her back for the finishing touch. She wore black patent slippers and black and green dangle earrings that accented her dress, plus an emerald ring that had belonged to her grandmother. She glanced once more in the mirror at her reflection and was pleased at what she saw.

When she started down the stairs, Tyree looked up and just stared at her. She was beautiful, and Tyree felt proud that she was going to be his wife. Emma noticed only Tyree. He was dressed in a black gabardine suit and a white western shirt with a black string tie and black boots. He was very handsome and Emma felt the love grow deeper for him.

Tyree came to the foot of the stairs and offered her his hand, and with a slight bow said, "Emma, may I have this dance?"

With a curtsy, Emma said, "Tyree, I will be proud to be your partner in this dance and all the dances to come."

Tyree guided her onto the dance floor that Riley had constructed for this occasion, took Emma in his arms and they danced together as if they had done this all their lives. It felt good to hold Emma, and he knew he would never let her go.

Tyree and Emma walked over to Uncle Alex after they finished their dance and Tyree said," Hey Uncle Alex, some Birthday party; the food is fantastic."

"You got that right Tyree," Uncle Alex said, "it was a surprise, and a real nice one at that!" At midnight the neighbors and friends started leaving so Emma started helping Cookie and Agatha to clean up. When everyone was gone, Emma went out and sat in the swing with Tyree. "Nice party," Emma commented. " I know Uncle Alex was surprised and pleased. I am glad also, as I have met a lot of nice people tonight, and everyone I talked to said they are looking forward to coming to our wedding."

"We will have a bigger wedding than what we had planned, Emma," said Tyree, "but I am glad that we will be surrounded by friends. You know, I think Riley had this figured out all along. It was nice of him along with Seth and Greg to throw this party for Uncle Alex, but I'll bet he was also thinking of our neighbors and friends meeting you. He can be a little sneaky like that."

"Well if he did it on purpose, I am glad, as I had a wonderful time, and Tyree, did you notice Seth and Maddie? If Seth isn't careful, he may get caught," said Emma gleefully.

Macee and Dave had just finished dancing and went to sit by Tyree and Emma. "Macee," said Emma, "you look beautiful this evening, and blue is very becoming on you." Macee had made her dress of a deep blue satin with white lace over the skirt and the yolk was scalloped at the neckline forming a vee. The bodice was snug fitting with the front of the waist forming a vee into the gathered skirt. The sleeves were blousy at the top, narrowing from the elbow down to the cuffs that were wide and snug fitting. "Thank you,

Emma," Macee told her, "and you look very lovely in green." "It's nice to have a party now and then," Dave said, "we'll have to do this more often."

As everyone was agreeing with him, Hildago rode up. "Nice party this evening," Hildago told them, "I really enjoyed myself." "It was nice, and we were just discussing having more parties in the future," Tyree said.

"I need to talk to you Tyree, if you can spare the time now," Hildago said, "it is important." "Excuse me Emma," Tyree said to her, "I'll be back before you retire." "I'll keep her company until you get back," Macee told him, "and we can talk about the wedding plans."

CHAPTER EIGHT

HILDAGO AND TYREE WALKED FROM the house and Hildago said, "Tyree, I know I have no right to ask, but I need your help. About two years ago, I met this man who came to me with authentic papers stating he had legally bought a ranch here in Keeline consisting of thirty thousand acres with all improvements brought up to date. This man knows Manuel Ortega, and he came out here over a year ago but I haven't heard from him, and now I am worried that something has happened to him. Since Manuel has been on Miss Emma's place, I thought if you would, ride with me to see Manuel."

"Sure thing, Hildago," Tyree said, "I'll be glad to help in any way I can. What is your friend's name?"

"His name is Chester Bain, and he is a land surveyor," Hildago told Tyree.

"How about we go first thing in the morning and visit Manuel and find out what he has to say," Tyree stated.

"Sounds great to me, and thanks Tyree," Hildago said.

When Tyree returned to the group on the veranda, he told them about his conversation with Hildago.

"Why not all of us go tomorrow, Tyree," stated Emma, "I would like Tam and Macee to help me with updating the furnishings in the house before the wedding. I asked Tam to meet us at my place around 9:00.

"Oh yes!" Macee implored. "And I can also speak for Tam that it will be most fun."

"That's settled then," Riley said, "since it is Sunday tomorrow we can have a fun day, and I'll ride into town and get Tam.

The next day proved to be sunny but with a brisk breeze. It was getting colder in the evenings and they knew they had a lot of work to do as winter was just around the corner. Uncle Alex, Seth and Greg came out to see them off, and Alex called to Tyree that he wanted a word with him.

"Tyree," Uncle Alex said, "I know I don't have to tell you that I am concerned about this land business that Hildago is investigating, and I also feel it involves Emma somehow." "I have been thinking of this also Uncle Alex, and I hope we are both wrong about our theories. I need to talk to Dave about his findings and I'll do it today and let you know," Tyree said.

"Okay Tyree, have a good time and we'll see you at supper time." Uncle Alex turned and walked back to the house.

As they rode down the lane, Tyree couldn't help but worry that Emma's property was involved in some kind of conspiracy. When they rode into the yard, Manuel came to the greet them.

"Hildago it is great to see you. It has been many years now since I was at your hacienda," Manuel told him. "Please, all of you come in and have coffee, and if you are hungry, I made fresh tamales this morning."

When they were all seated and enjoying the coffee and tamales, Emma said, "Manuel, with the help of Tam and Macee, I plan to update the furnishings in the house before the wedding, so I hope we will not get in your way, and I need to tell you that Riley and Tam will be here any minute."

"Oh, Senorita Emma, you plan to be married here?"

asked Manuel. "Yes, we want to be married here, very much, Manuel, and then we plan to live here."

"That is what I have wished for," remarked Manuel, "it has been a long time you have been away, and now it is time for you to return home."

Hildago asked the men to step outside with him, and then he said, "Manuel, I know you have had problems here, but can you tell me why you sent for me in particular? Tyree, Riley, Dave and the others could have helped you with whatever problem there is."

"No, Hildago," Manuel stated, "they couldn't help with what we have to face. I know you have been involved with Spanish Land Grants, and in order for Senorita Emma to keep her place, we will need to go over all the documents very carefully. You have also been appointed a delegate to the Spanish Land Grant Committee, so we need your expertise in this matter. As you know, Senorita Emma's father is of Spanish descendent as her Grandfather was born and raised in Spain."

"Do you know where the Spanish Land Grants are Manuel, and have you looked at them?" asked Hildago.

"Yes, I have them, as Senor Cain gave them to me to keep them safe. I think he knew that something was going to happen to him, and I know he wanted Senorita Emma to come home and run the ranch," Manuel told them.

Tyree then asked Dave what he found when he studied the deed to Emma's ranch. "First of all," Dave said, "I found no discrepancies' in the deed itself. It is all legal and signed, witnessed and has the state seal stamped on the document. I found no mention of the Spanish Land Grant, so I presume we should look at these documents as soon as possible. Manuel, you and Hildago come to my office tomorrow at around ten in the morning and bring the documents."

"We'll be there Dave, and thanks." Hildago said. When the men joined the women again, they got caught up in the plans for the refurnishing of the house, and then Emma told them that Tyree and she would announce their wedding date during supper.

After planning some more for the wedding, it was late afternoon and they told Manuel they had to leave. "Manuel," Emma told him, "I'll be back tomorrow to rearrange the furniture, and I have bought material for new curtains and Macee said she would make them for me, and Tam is helping with the color themes. We'll bring lunch for all of us, so don't go to any trouble cooking."

After they left, Manuel stood in the doorway for a long time thinking how nice it would be to have Senorita Emma and her new husband, Tyree living here. Cain and Lois Reed would be very happy about Emma's choice for a husband and to be coming home to live. As he was watching the sunset, he quickly turned his head, as he saw some movement from the corner of his eye.

The house was dark, so he was not out-lined in the doorway. He stepped quietly back into the house and stood there watching. It was a good fifteen minutes before he saw the movement again. It was an outline of a man, and as Manuel watched, the man backed away from the spot where he was crouched disappearing into the arroyo. Manuel quietly closed the door and without lighting the lamp, made sure the house was secure then went to his room and retired for the night. He knew he would go to the spot in the morning and see if he could find tracks or anything that would help identify the man.

After Tyree and Dave had unsaddled and the horses were taken care of, they washed up for supper. Riley rode with Tam back to town, and told Tyree he was taking Tam to supper in town.

After everyone was seated at the table, Emma announced that their wedding day was planned for May Fifth. She also told them that this would be enough time for her to plan for her dress, and hoped that Macee would make it for her.

"Oh, Emma!" gasped Macee, "I would be honored to make your dress. I will send off for the material this coming week. I can't wait to get started."

Tyree then asked Seth, Greg and Dave to be his Groomsmen, and Riley to be his best man. Emma asked Macee if she would be her maid of honor and Tam her bridesmaid. She would also ask Maddie to be a bridesmaid.

Emma turned to Uncle Alex and said, "Uncle Alex, since my father is gone, I would very much like you to give me away, if you wouldn't mind."

He was so overwhelmed he had to look away and clear his throat. "I will be more than honored Emma to give you away," Uncle Alex told her.

With that being settled, they finished their meal in silence and they all were hoping for the best about Emma's ranch.

Manuel woke early and as the coffee perked, he dressed and made sure the house was tidy for Emma and the girls. He filled his cup and put on his sheep skin coat and went to the spot where the man had been hiding. He found where the grass had been trampled and it looked as if this had been several different times. He also found several stubs of brown cigarettes scattered around, and they did not look to be American made.

He found the track of a big boot, and the impression of the boot indicated a big man. He would be sure to tell Dave and Hildago what he found. When Manuel returned to the house he heard a horse coming down the lane and looking out saw it was Hildago.

"Morning Manuel," Hildago said, "ready to go?"

"As soon as I saddle up, we'll go," Manuel told him.

Before leaving the house, Manuel stuck a small piece of paper between the door and door jam, and then shut the door and locked it. Hildago saw this, but did not comment, as he knew Manuel would talk of his actions sooner or later. They rode to town in silence, each with their own thoughts and as they rode to Dave's office, they noticed a big Spanish looking man on a big beautiful black Arabian horse riding toward them.

When they came abreast, Manuel noticed the cigarette in the man's mouth was the same color as the one he found on the ground, and the intense glare the man gave Manuel made Manuel uneasy. Manuel also noticed the man's powerful arms and then he became aware that Hildago also noticed. "Do you know this man Manuel?" asked Hildago.

"No I have never met him or seen him before, and I do not think I want to know him," Manuel told Hildago.

They dismounted in front of Dave's office just as the church bell was pronouncing ten o'clock. When they entered, they were impressed with the furnishings of the office. The big desk was made of cherry wood with big easy chairs for clients to sit in. File cabinets lined one wall and book shelves with law books located behind Dave's chair. As Manuel and Hildago sat in the easy chairs, Dave offered them coffee and they gratefully accepted as it had been a chilly ride in.

Manuel handed Dave the Spanish Land Grants and then as Dave spread them out on the oval table situated in the corner of the room, he asked Hildago and Manuel to join him as he needed them to translate for him. As Hildago was reading the legal documents, there was no mention of Spanish Land Grants for Keeline, Wyoming. The ranch was legally Emma's, and if there was anyone that wanted to challenge the fact, the courts would have to be involved. The way the Grants were written, was that Emma's Grandfather had possession first. He then legally purchased the land from Spain and when he had full possession, went to the County Seat and had the United States draw up the deeds as this would clinch the deal on the ranch. As far as the three men could determine everything was in order and legal.

Dave was relieved and would be glad to tell Emma the news. Manuel then spoke up and told Dave and Hildago of a man he saw last night after everyone had left, but couldn't identify him, and of finding the boot print and the brown cigarette butt when he went to investigate this morning. He also told them of passing this man when he and Hildago were riding into town.

"Can you describe him to me Manuel?" asked Dave.

"Si, I think so," said Manuel, "he is a very big man with a black beard and he has dark black hair that I saw under his sombrero. I think he is Spanish, and he wears a leather black jacket. He rides a big beautiful black Arabian horse. He smokes cigarettes that are not made here in the States and his eyes are very evil and angry looking."

"We'll go see Sheriff John Madison and see if he knows anything about this man," Dave stated, "but first, let's go to the Trail's End Café for lunch."

As they were leaving Dave's office, Jed Peterson was crossing the street.

"Hey Jed," shouted Dave "Want to have lunch with us?"

"Don't mind if I do," stated Jed. When they were seated and had ordered, Dave introduced Hildago to Jed.

"Nice meeting you, Hildago," Jed told him. "What brings you to this part of the country?"

Hildago explained to Jed about the Spanish Land Grant and about the man. After describing the man, Hildago asked Jed if he had seen him. "No, I haven't," replied Jed, "but do you suppose he thinks these Spanish Land Grants are legal here and he somehow is related to Emma's father?"

"By golly, Jed," exclaimed Dave, "you might have something there. I didn't give it a thought, but then I only heard about him this morning. I think I had better investigate this more and wire the County Seat about the possibility of anyone asking about the Spanish Land Grants. Thanks for the heads up!"

"Anytime Dave, anytime," said Jed.

After lunch, Manuel and Hildago left to return to Emma's place while Dave headed for the telegraph office. He didn't notice the big man watching him, and if he had, wouldn't have liked the look on the man's face.

When Dave walked into the telegraph office, Lewis Morgan looked up and with a smile said, "looks like you have been busy today, Dave."

"I have been Lewis, and now I need to send this telegraph to the County Seat." He handed Lewis the paper reading: Need to know if anyone in the last two weeks have been inquiring about Spanish Land Grants. If so, please telegraph me back with name (if possible) and description. Please reply soon. Dave Steele, Lawyer. Keeline, Wyoming.

"Thanks Lewis," Dave said. "I'll stop in tomorrow and see if I have an answer. Dave walked back to his office and after tidying up decided to close for the day as it was almost three thirty.

After locking up he walked to the livery and as he was saddling his horse, Frank Gates the livery owner came in.

"Howdy Dave," said Frank, "saw you had some clients today, so hope your business is doing well."

"It is a little slow," Dave told him, "but I think when word gets around about my business I will be able to expand."

"Sure thing, Dave, and I'll help spread the word for you." "Thanks Frank, I appreciate that."

Dave mounted and headed toward the Rocking S, not knowing that a man on a big black Arabian horse was following, but keeping to shadows and off the trail.

When Dave rode into the yard, Macee ran out to meet him. "I missed you today, Dave Steele," she stated.

"Same here Macee," Dave told her as he took her in his arms and planted a solid kiss on her upturned lips. As he looked up after kissing Macee, he saw the big man on the big black Arabian horse sitting there glaring at them. Dave softly told Macee to go to the house and tell Tyree and Riley to come out, and to be cautious.

Macee turned and ran to the house, and as she did so, the big man drew his gun and fired at Dave! Dave's reaction was slow, as he wasn't expecting anything like this to happen, and above all the stranger gave no warning. The bullet missed Dave by a hair, but hit Macee.

Tyree and Riley heard the shot and came running out. Tyree tripped over Macee, and as he was getting up, saw Dave draw his gun and shoot the big man. As the man was falling, Riley ran over to him, but knew he was dead.

Dave ran to Macee and saw the bullet had grazed the top of her right shoulder. He picked her up and carried her to the living room where he laid her on the couch. Emma was waiting with a blanket and went to the cabinet where she retrieved the bottle of whiskey and hot water along with clean bandages. Macee was still unconscious, so Emma hurried and cleaned and bandaged the wound as this would be easier for Macee to endure. Dave sat with Macee and thanked God that Macee would be alright.

When Tyree and Riley came in to see how Macee was getting along, Dave explained about the big man he had killed, hoping to have a name soon and that he was looking into the matter of the Spanish Land Grants that Manuel and Hildago had dropped off.

After everyone had gone to bed, Dave sat with Macee to be sure she was comfortable, and when she woke she wouldn't be alone. He had dozed off and something had awakened him.

It was a moonlit night and when his eyes finally adjusted to the semi-darkness noticed that Macee was awake and looking at him. "Hey, Macee," Dave said softly. "Are you in pain?" "Can I get you anything?"

"What happened, Dave?" Macee asked. "The last thing

I remember I started to the house and then everything went black."

Dave explained to her about the big man and that he killed him as he had no choice. "We'll talk more tomorrow, Macee," Dave told her, "right now you need rest, and I will be right here for you. I love you Macee and I realize that more now as I could have lost you."

"Oh Dave," Macee stated, "I will never leave you and I will always love you. Sleep well and don't worry about me."

Dave bent over Macee and kissed her goodnight then settled back in the easy chair where he went to sleep and slept soundly.

The sun was just peeking over the mountain tops when Macee said, "Dave, I am sorry you had to kill that man, and I know you had it to do, but now we'll never find out where he is from or why he came here."

"I know Macee," replied Dave, "I have been thinking on that and when I go into town today, I will wire Uncle Lane with what has happened and also will describe the man's looks. Maybe Uncle Lane has something on him in the Pinkerton files."

"I want to go with you today Dave, because I need to get my shop ready for business. The final papers for the lease are ready for you to look over, and hopefully everything is in order for my signature," Macee said. "Are you feeling well enough to do all the things you want to do today, Macee?" implored Dave.

"I think if you feel you need to, you better wear a sling to help support your shoulder. I know the bullet cut a pretty deep gash; if you start moving it a lot, you're liable to open the wound and start bleeding." "I'll do as you ask Dave," Macee said, "and also, when we left Emma's the other day, I mentioned to Tam about the plans I made for today and she wants to help me. I told her I would be at the shop at nine this morning."

"In that case, I won't worry too much about you Macee, but just don't overdue and rest a lot," Dave exclaimed.

Tyree and Riley came in to see how Macee was feeling and both were relieved to see her sitting up drinking coffee that Dave brought her. "Looks like you are doing great Macee," Tyree said, "I am sure glad." "Goes for me also sis," Riley told her. "You gave us a scare."

"I am feeling fine and I intend to go into town, with Dave's permission, and start cleaning the shop. Tam is coming to help me, so I won't have to do any heavy lifting."

She glanced at Riley when she mentioned Tam's name and he got red in the face and looked away. Macee chuckled to herself and then said, "Why don't you meet us for lunch at the Trail's End Café, say around noon."

Riley looked at Tyree and Dave and said that would be great and turned and walked quickly from the room. They all laughed to see Riley so flustered and pleased he liked Tam so much.

Emma appeared in the doorway and after they explained what they were laughing about, she grinned at them agreeing it would be great if Riley and Tam became involved.

After everyone left the room, Macee got up and dressed and then went to the dining room where the others were already seated waiting for breakfast. Uncle Alex, Seth, Trey and Greg talked of their plans for the day. The first thing Uncle Alex said was that Riley should saddle up and take the body to town on the pack horse. His first stop would be to report to Sheriff Madison, then stop at the morticians to talk to Bain Black about making arrangements for the burial. Dave said he hoped to have word back this day from his Uncle Lane about the dead man, and if he had any relatives.

"If you're ready Macee," Dave said, "I'll go hitch up the buggy as I don't think you should be riding horseback today."

"I am ready, Dave," Macee said, "I just have to get a few things and I will meet you out front."

With the help of Seth and Tyree the three men put the man's body on the pack horse. Riley waited until Macee was in the buggy and as Dave started the horses, Riley rode his horse leading the pack horse. When they reached town, Dave stopped at Macee's shop and helped her down. Tam was already there and ran to Macee as she noticed that Macee was wearing a sling. Macee was explaining to Tam about the shooting when Tam looked up and saw Riley coming down the road.

She waved and smiled at him and he stopped in front of her and said, "Tam, would you like to have lunch with me today?" "I would be pleased to have lunch with you," she replied.

"I'll come and pick you up at noon," Riley told her.

"Mind if Dave and I join you?" asked Macee.

"That would be fine," Riley said and then he rode on to the jail where he spotted Sheriff Madison sitting on the bench in front of the jail reading a paper." Hey, Riley," said Sheriff Madison, "looks like you had a little trouble. "Actually, Sheriff, Dave did," Riley exclaimed. "Yesterday this fellow followed Dave back to the ranch and Dave didn't have a chance, as this man just drew and fired on Dave. The bullet meant for Dave hit Macee, and luckily it just grazed the top of her shoulder. She will be fine. We have no idea who this gunman is, but Dave is telegraphing his Uncle right now and hopefully the Pinkerton's can help in identifying him. We have no clue as to where he came from, or why he came here. I thought I better stop here first to see you before I went to the morticians."

"Let me look at him, and see if I have seen him around," Sheriff Madison Said. As Riley uncovered the man's face, Sheriff Madison shook his head. "No, I haven't seen him before, but maybe he didn't come here alone. I would keep my eyes open for strangers Riley, and I'll do the same. I'll pass the word also to look especially for anyone that has Spanish features."

"Thanks Sheriff," Riley told him, "I appreciate that."

Riley then headed for the mortuary and Bain Black came to greet him. "Have some business for you Bain," Riley said, "but I don't know his name. Dave is trying to locate relatives of his, but have no idea how long that will take."

"Okay Riley," Bain said, "I will just go ahead and build the casket so he can be buried in the cemetery with a blank marker for now. We can put his name on later when his relatives are located."

Riley and Bain carried the man inside and Riley told Bain he would pay whatever expenses Bain incurred.

"We'll discuss that later Riley," said Bain.

CHAPTER NINE

RILEY WALKED TO MACEE'S SHOP and when he entered he noticed Tam was struggling with the desk.

"Here, let me help you Tam," Riley said, "where do you want it put?" "Over by the window," Macee told him. "I feel so helpless with this darn shoulder!" she exclaimed.

"Just take it easy Macee," Riley told her, "I will be glad to stay and help you girls today."

"Thanks Riley," Macee said, "I hate to see Tam having to wrestle all this heavy furniture."

The girls and Riley had been working for three hours when Dave came in and suggested they stop for lunch. After they had washed up, they walked to the Trail's End Café, and as they entered they saw Seth and Maddie in deep conversation at the far end of the dining room. Macee motioned to the others to sit at the table farthest from Maddie and Seth. When they were seated, Macee said, "I don't want to interfere right now, but we will ask Maddie if she would like to help us at the shop this afternoon. I really like her."

"I do too," Tam said, "we could use her ideas also for Emma's wedding. I would like to include her in our plans, to let her know we would like to be her friends."

"I agree Tam, and I think it is a wonderful idea. She must be lonely since her father has died," Macee said.

"Well Maddie, I hope things have settled down for you now as you have your father's estate closed," Seth said."

"It has been a long drawn out procedure, but the estate is finally settled." "Father left me the ranch, with Jeffrey being taken care of. As you know, Jeffrey was living with my father, and I didn't want to change that as I know Jeffrey was close to my father. I have set up a trust fund for Jeffrey, and this year when we brand, Jeffrey will have two calves branded for him, and every year from now on two calves will be added to his herd. This is what father wanted and I will carry out his wishes," Maddie told him, "and also I am fortunate that the hands who worked for father said they would be glad to stay and work for me. That means a lot, as some men wouldn't consider working for a woman. I will admit I don't know much about ranching, but my foreman is on top of things."

"If you need help Maddie, I would help anyway I can," Seth told her.

"I will hold you to that Seth," Maddie told him. "Oh, there is Macee with Tam, Dave and Riley. I wonder what they are doing today," Maddie pondered.

"I do know the girls are cleaning Macee's shop today, and Riley brought a dead man to Bain. This man followed Dave home yesterday, threw down on him, and Dave had to kill him. The bullet that was meant for Dave hit Macee and grazed the top of her shoulder, but she will be alright," Seth told Maddie.

"Why would anyone want to shoot Dave, and does anyone know this man?" asked Maddie.

"No, we don't know his name or anything about him," Seth said, "but Dave wired his Uncle Lane and hopefully he can find out about this person. We do know he is Spanish, but that is all."

The waiter brought their food and they ate in silence, each wondering about the shooting that took place at the Rocking S Ranch.

Macee looked over to where Seth and Maddie were sitting, and when she caught Maddie's eye, she smiled and gave a little wave. Maddie waved and smiled back. The waitress brought the food to Macee's table and they settled down to eating. After Seth and Maddie finished their meal, they walked over to the table where Macee was sitting. "Nice seeing all of you," Maddie told them.

"You too, Maddie," Macee told her. "You know, if you aren't too busy this afternoon, why not stay and visit." "After we eat we are going back to my shop and clean some more. We would love to have you join us."

"I have to be getting back to the ranch," Seth said to Maddie, "but I will be out to see you soon."

"I will be looking forward to your visit, Seth," Maddie said with a grin, "and I will be glad to join your cleaning crew Macee."

Maddie had coffee as the others finished eating and she was glad they were including her. She didn't realize how lonely she had been until now. It would be great to start a new life here and hopefully she would find the courage to tell Jeffrey about his birth right. She hadn't heard back from Jacob McFadden and it had been three weeks ago she had wired about Jeffrey.

When they arrived at the shop Tam told Maddie she was glad she decided to join them. Macee said that she would like to start cleaning the back room as she planned to put a bed, dresser, and a stove there. "This way I will have a place to stay if the weather gets bad or if I have late customers," said Macee.

"Sounds like a real good plan," Tam said. Maddie grabbed the broom and started sweeping while Macee measured the windows for blinds and curtains. Tam was moving an easy chair into the room when there was a knock at the door. Macee opened the door and there was a young lady with a little girl.

"Hello," Macee said, "what can I do for you?"

"My name is Sheri Finch and this is my daughter Bree. We just arrived this morning and staying at the Montreal Boarding House. I was wondering if you knew of any empty buildings that I could purchase or rent. I am planning to open a bakery here."

"Come in Sheri and sit for a spell," Macee said, "how about a cup of tea?"

"That sounds great," replied Sheri, "it was early this morning that we had refreshments and we are a little parched."

As they entered the shop, Macee introduced Sheri and Bree to Tam and Maddie. When they were enjoying their tea and small cakes that Maddie had brought, Macee asked Sheri where she and Bree had come from.

"Bree and I lived in Sacramento, California, and then Bree's father passed away three months ago. He left us financially well off, but I couldn't stay there, so I sold the ranch and through some of my friends telling me about Keeline, I packed up Bree and here we are. So far what I have seen and the people I have met, I am impressed. I also have heard that the school is rated high, and that Maddie is an excellent teacher. That means a lot to me."

As they were finishing their tea and cakes, Riley and Alex rode up. When they stopped at Macee's shop, she ran out and hurried them inside.

"I want you to meet Sheri Finch and her daughter Bree," Macee said. "Hello, I am Alex Skylar, Macee and Riley's Uncle. There is one more Skylar that goes by Tyree."

"I am glad to meet you," stated Sheri.

"Likewise," Uncle Alex told her. "So what brings you here to Keeline?" asked Riley.

Sheri explained to Alex and Riley why she came, and that she was interested in opening a bakery.

"There is an empty building at the end of the street,"

stated Alex, "it was used to store stock feed, but the owner moved to Laramie and no one else took over the business. It has been empty for quite a spell and I don't know what condition it is in. I am sure there are rodents living there and Lord knows what else. If you want, I can bring some of my hands in and we can see what needs to be done to make it livable while turning it into a bakery. We need to have people like you to help the town grow."

"I will appreciate all the help I can get," Sheri told Alex, "and in the meantime if Mrs. Montreal wouldn't mind, I could start making cakes, pies, cookies and breads in her kitchen."

"I tell you what, Mrs. Finch," said Alex," if Miss Montreal won't let you use her kitchen, you come out to the Rocking S and I know Cookie wouldn't mind sharing the kitchen."

"Thank you so very much, Mr. Skylar," Sheri said, "if I have to, I'll take you up on that offer."

"Let's go over and take a look at the old feed store and see what needs to be done," Riley said.

Sheri asked Macee if Bree could stay with her for a little while as she wanted to see what the building was like. Macee was glad to keep Bree, so Sheri went with Riley and Alex.

As they approached the old feed store, Sheri was having reservations about starting a bakery. What if she failed? What if people didn't buy her baked goods, and could she fix the building up to be livable? All these thoughts were going through her mind when Riley opened the big door and they stepped inside. What Sheri saw surprised her and she stood in awe at how clean everything looked in spite of the building being empty for so long. There were several rooms off the big room that would make great living quarters.

The floors were wood and in good condition, and the walls were okay. The windows were big and let in a lot of light, so she would make curtains. Riley and Alex were both amazed at how well the inside looked.

"Seems like it will take a little fixing up Mrs. Finch," Alex told her, "I will be glad to help you clean up and don't hesitate to ask me for anything." "Thank you Mr. Skylar," Sheri said.

"If you don't mind, Mrs. Finch," said Alex, "I would like us to be on a first name basis. I don't like to be called "Mr." "That will be fine with me," Sheri told him, "as I don't like to be called "Mrs." as it makes me feel old."

Riley came back into the big room and told them the other rooms were in good shape also. He also stated that they would be big enough for a living room, kitchen and two bedrooms.

"I will need to contact the owner and find out the cost and hopefully I can start moving in and start my business," Sheri told them.

"If you want, I can ask Dave to contact the owner and if the price is right, I am sure Dave will draw up the legal papers for you," said Riley. "I really appreciate your help, both of you," stated Sheri, "and anytime you come to town, stop in for a free treat."

When Riley said he was going back to Macee's shop, Uncle Alex said he would stay and help Sheri decide what rooms she should make into the bedrooms. She decided to have tables and chairs in the big room as she had plans for serving tea and cakes in the afternoons, as this would be good advertisement for her business.

Since it was close to supper time, Alex asked Sheri if she and Bree would join him at the Trail's End Café. She accepted and they walked to Macee's shop to pick up Bree.

"Well Sheri," asked Macee, "have you decided what you want to do?" Sheri told them of her plans and the women thought it sounded great. Maddie excused herself as she needed to get home to get supper for Jeffrey and her foreman. "I will be at the school tomorrow if you need me," Maddie said.

Maddie woke with the sun warming her face. She lay snuggled under the covers and thought of what the day would be like. This was the day she was going to tell Jeffrey about his heritage. She was sure he was old enough to understand and was more mature than most boys his age. She was not going to hold anything back, and she how hard this was going to be for both of them.

She hurriedly dressed and went down the stairs quietly so Jeffrey could sleep a little longer while she got the stove stoked and make the coffee. She always marveled at this house her father built.

Her parents had been hard working people and her father came from a long line of carpenters. The house was built of logs, with a wooden floor. There were four bedrooms, a large dining room, living room and a big kitchen with lots of windows and a breezeway. Off the living room was the parlor.

As she entered the kitchen, she was surprised to see Jeffrey had started the fire in the cook stove and had coffee brewing. She went to the door and noticed Jeffrey was getting wood. He looked up and saw her, smiled and said, "I hope the coffee will taste okay. I used to make it for grandpa and he never complained, so I don't know if it is good."

"I think it will taste just fine," Maddie told him. After Jeffrey had stacked the wood in the kitchen, he went to the cupboard and took down two cups. He went to the stove and poured the coffee for Maddie first. He waited until she had tasted the coffee, nodded it was good then poured himself a cup.

"Jeffrey," Maddie said, " sit with me at the table. I need to tell you something and please don't interrupt until I have finished." "Sounds pretty serious to me," Jeffrey told her. "It is Jeffrey, and I really hope this comes out the way it should."

"I need you to know that I am your mother. I have been

a coward all these years and I am so sorry that I haven't been here for you. You see, I fell in love, and we were to be married. The same day I found out I was pregnant with you your father came to me and told me he enlisted in the war. I was devastated. He never gave me a chance to say anything and just rode off. He never knew about you. I heard he had been killed in the war, so my parents helped me. Father, your granddad, sold our place in Ohio and sent me to Philadelphia to wait for your birth then he and your grandma went on to Wyoming to buy land. When they settled here, they came to Philadelphia and brought you back here to live with them. I stayed, attended school and studied to become a teacher."

"After your grandma passed away, I wanted to take you back East with me, but Father said he couldn't bear to give you up, so we agreed for you to live on here. When father wired me of his illness, I came as soon as I could. I had to find someone to take over my classes, and I then heard that a teaching job was open here, so I applied and was fortunate to be hired."

Jeffrey sat there staring down at his hands. Maddie noticed a tear fall in his lap, but she didn't say anything. She wanted her words to soak in and so she gave him his space. After a couple of minutes Jeffrey looked up at her with tears streaming down his face. "I have waited for you for so long," he said quietly, "and every day I prayed you would come. Grandpa told me you would be coming, but I really had my doubts."

"Oh Jeffrey, I have loved you always, and I wanted so much to tell you before, but I didn't know if you could have taken it all in."

"So, is my Father dead?" Jeffrey asked her.

"No, he is alive," she told him. "You know Tam McFadden, Jeffrey. She is your Aunt. Your father is Jacob McFadden, and he lives now in Hardin, Montana. I wired him about you, but he never wired back."

"He may not want to know about me," Jeffrey said, "but I don't think it matters that much. You are the one that had the courage to have me. I heard grandpa talk about a lot of kids that went to the orphanage because their parents didn't want them, or couldn't care for them. So mom, I guess we're stuck with each other."

With a cry of joy and tears running down her face, Maddie knelt in front of Jeffrey and with hugs and kisses she thanked her lucky stars for this mature twelve year old boy. She silently thanked her parents for raising Jeffrey to be a responsible person.

When Maddie finally had her emotions under control, she said, "Jeffrey, I can't wait to tell the world about you. I am so proud of you and I promise you no one will ever come between us." "I feel the same way mom, and now how about some breakfast, I am starved!"

"Jeffrey, I need to go to town today and stop at the school. I I need to put together the lessons for Monday. You can come with me or stay here and help feed the animals. We'll have a special supper tonight to celebrate our reunion."

"I think I will stay here," Jeffrey said. "I will help the foreman with the chores, because someday I will take grandpa's place."

Maddie cleaned up the kitchen and after freshening up, went to the barn to hitch up the buggy. Jeffrey was waiting for her and with the foreman's help had the buggy ready in no time. Maddie couldn't believe how fortunate she was and she knew Jeffrey felt the same way.

After she had the lessons ready for Monday, she stopped at the butcher's and picked up a smoked ham. She then headed for home with a much lighter heart. It was around five p.m. when she stopped in front of the ranch house. She sat there and breathed in the beauty of her ranch. Jeffrey came out and helped her down, and after taking the groceries in he drove the buggy to the barn where he and the foreman unhitched the horse. Jeffrey led the horse to water then put him in the corral where he forked hay to him.

When he returned to the house he heard his mother humming softly while preparing the meal for supper. Her back was to him, and as he was about to say something to her she started quoting a poem.

End of Day

When the sun starts to go down,
And you walk in the twilight of the moon,
The reflections of the wonderful life you have
With your loved ones come back to you;
It is easy to overcome the turmoil of the day
And to help your feelings soothe;
It is comforting to know that you're not alone in
This world of confusion and to be able to talk,
Laugh and play with open mind with no illusions.
Doris Miller

When Maddie turned from the stove she saw Jeffrey standing there with a big grin on his face. "Mom, we are going to be fine and I want you to know I always prayed that you would be my mother." Maddie took him in her arms and held him tight.

"I guess we had better get this food on the table and eat it before it gets any later," Maddie told him. After the dishes were washed and kitchen cleaned, Jeffrey went up to bed. Maddie went to the living room and was sitting in front of the fireplace preparing lessons for the next day. There was a light tap on the door and when Maddie opened the door, she was surprised to see Seth standing there.

"Hi Seth," Maddie said. "What brings you here this time of night?" "I was on my way home from town and I decided to stop by and say hello. I hope it isn't too late,"

Seth said. "Please, come in. Can I get you a cup of coffee? It is still hot from supper," Maddie said. "Sounds great if it is no bother," Seth said. "Please, sit down and I'll fetch the coffee," Maddie told him. Seth took off his hat and hung it on the peg by the door. He sat at the kitchen table and was admiring the craftsmanship that Maddie's father put into building the house. He wished he could have met her parents.

Maddie set two cups of steaming coffee on the table and then asked Seth if he would like a piece of pie. "You bet!" he replied. She went to the cupboard and cut a big slice and set it in front of him. "Sure looks delicious," Seth told her. She watched him as he ate the pie and smiled to herself knowing he was thoroughly enjoying every bite. He didn't look up and no words were spoken as he ate. When he finished, he sighed with contentment and sat back in his chair. With a big smile he said, "Maddie, you are a darned good cook. That was the best apple pie I have ever eaten. Thanks."

"Is everything alright with you Seth?" Maddie asked him. "Just fine Maddie, but I need to ask you a question," Seth said. "Okay, Seth," she replied, "what is it you want to ask?" "I have a horse that I want to give to Jeffrey, but I needed to ask you first before I said anything to Jeffrey. The horse is a bay gelding three years old. He is gentle and would make Jeffrey a great horse. What do you say Maddie?" Maddie looked at Seth with tears in her eyes. "Oh Seth, "I think that is wonderful of you. Jeffrey will be overwhelmed as I am," she said. "I'll bring him over tomorrow and they can start getting acquainted. By the way, his name is Andy, but if Jeffrey wants to change the name he can," Seth said.

Maddie refreshed their coffee and then she said, "Seth I need to tell you about Jeffrey. It isn't going to be easy telling you this, but I have grown fond of you and your friendship means a lot to me. Jeffrey is my son and I told him this morning and you should have seen the joy and relief on his face. I feel fortunate that he accepts the fact." She went on to tell Seth the whole story. After she finished Seth said, "I know it must have been hard on you, but Maddie, you did the right thing and I am proud of you. You and Jeffrey mean a lot to me, and I would like to be a big part in your lives if you will let me. Also wire Jacob McFadden again, and this time if he doesn't answer, we'll make plans for our future with Jeffrey." "Seth, I would love to have you in our lives," she told him. Seth got up and pulled Maddie into his arms and sealed the deal with a kiss. "I'll see you tomorrow after school and bring Andy over as a surprise to Jeffrey." "Goodnight Seth, until tomorrow night."

After Seth left, Maddie sat there for a long time letting everything that happened this day sink in. She went upstairs to her room and after turning the lamp down she got into bed and thanked God for this wonderful day.

Seth was overjoyed at how things went with Maddie and him. When he reached the Rocking S ranch, he hurriedly watered and fed his horse. Everyone was in the living room having coffee when he entered. "Looks like you have something on your mind Seth," Riley said. "Yeah Seth," Uncle Alex said. "You remind me of the cat that ate the bird." "For your information, Alex, I have just come from visiting Maddie, and boy she makes a mean apple pie," Seth replied. "Looks as though you swallowed a love bug on the way home," Tyree said. Everyone was grinning at him, but they all knew he had feelings for Maddie and hoped things would work out for them.

"Guess we better turn in because we have a big day ahead of us. We need to bring the cows closer to home, as winter is upon us. We will be calving soon, and we need to check them every day and start feeding them hay," Uncle Alex told them.

Macee reminded them that Christmas was in three weeks, and she was making plans for Christmas dinner and making invitations to send out to close friends. Riley told her he would bring home the tree he had spotted earlier in the year for her to decorate.

After everyone said goodnight, Macee went over to Seth and told him she was very glad for him and Maddie. "Thank you Macee," Seth told her. "Maddie is a good person Seth," Macee said, "I know she will make you a good wife, when you two decide to tie the knot." "Good night Seth," Macee said.